By Martha Gellhorn

The Heart of Another

The Heart of Another

By
MARTHA GELLHORN

NEW YORK

Charles Scribner's Sons

1941

For
Hortense Flexner
and
Wyncie King

Contents

The Heart of Another

The heart of another is a dark forest.

Luigi's House

THE WOMAN stood on the doorstep and looked at the stringy dahlias and the roses in the garden and beyond them to the small candelabra vines. Flies hummed about her, swollen and lazy, dying with the summer. From time to time a breeze came through the eucalyptus trees; the sea was two kilometers away. There were good clean rock mountains against the sky to the left of the house.

I wanted a home, she thought, and now I have one. She turned and saw the three mimosa trees and the old well and the rusty gate. It takes a little time to get used to a home, she told herself. Perhaps it is the silence. She lit a cigarette and sat down on the doorstep.

If you could always choose, probably you would not choose Corsica. But you followed your man wherever he had to go; you stayed near him or waited close by: there was nothing strange in that. And if you were lucky enough to have any time the way the world went, moving disastrously between wars, you made a home wherever you could. We will have had a home this once even if it does not last, she thought, and that is enough. It is all I want, a home for us together, now.

But her mind was still in the places she had been before: her mind and her body remembered only the trains, boats, planes, cars, customs sheds, the always worn-looking hotel rooms in the cities you never really know. She lived still with the war she had seen in the cold blind streets of Madrid where first you heard the shells landing loud round and close between the buildings, and then you heard the breaking glass; in Aragon, your face stiff with dust, your eyes red and hot with it, and the war spread out and quieter in the width of the land; on the low cool empty hills above Morata; at Tortosa beside the dangling bridges over the Ebro. Her mind was still tormented with that war and she feared what would come next, knowing that no matter what, war or peace, there was very little time left for people to live as they should, in their own house, watching the days go past.

Luigi came up the path from the vines, walked past her and did not speak. She said *bon jour* to him and he looked away. Probably the American woman was not wicked but what she had done was wicked; or else it was Signoret, the owner, who was a criminal and a thief. They had done it together anyhow because they could read and sign papers with the lawyer. He went into the kitchen. There were the same things to think and his mind was sick with them and there was no rest in the vines. A man could not work and worry. It was his house, his land. He had lived here for eleven years and every year he had taken the grapes to the cellar and made the wine and then Signoret got half the money and he kept the rest and next year was like last year. Signoret came down from his village in the hills at the end of the summer and helped with the grapes but otherwise Luigi was alone, the way he wanted to be.

Then there was this American woman who had walked up the road one afternoon (and he had opened the gate but he was a fool to open the gate; he should have hidden in the house and waited for her to go away). She looked at the house. Luigi had never thought about the house at all and she came and said it was filthy, the water did not work, the paint was dirty, there were cockroaches, and in the kitchen she wrinkled her nose and went quickly out of doors. He had told her that Signoret owned the farm and three days later she came back and said that Signoret had rented the farm to her, she was going to clean it up. ("It will be much more comfortable, Luigi." He did not want to be comfortable. He was comfortable as he was, alone.)

Signoret had said—when Luigi found him in the town —"I am sure you will make an arrangement with the lady; she is most obliging." But who is master here, Luigi thought; without me the land would fail and must I take orders from the woman?

The proprietor had explained to the woman that Luigi must stay on because of the farm itself, the vines, and

3

besides it was well to have a man in the house—a man of all confidence—since the property was so far away from the town and so alone. Of course, Signoret had said, he will do as you say and sleep in the little room over the kitchen. (At the moment Luigi slept all over the house, all the beds half made and dank gray, his clothes strewn like rotting leaves through the rooms; the smell of the dirty kitchen, with the greasy piled dishes and the clogged drains, followed him.)

Luigi came out of the house.

"Are you going to stay?" he said.

"Naturally." Why does he have to behave like this, she thought.

"Where will you sleep?"

"I won't sleep here at all until the place is cleaned. The painter will be out tomorrow. I think it will take about ten days to fix it up. Please move your things into your own room, so that he can start to work."

Luigi did not seem to hear her.

The painter, a big man with curling eyelashes and Left ideas, was in a temper.

"If Luigi will not move his things, how am I to work, Madame? You must consider that I have the two assistants to pay and part of the day already lost. Who owns this farm, in the end?"

She went to Luigi among the vines and was careful of

4

her voice. If I begin shouting at him, she thought, all is lost. She sat down and Luigi stared at her angrily as if she were bruising the earth, his earth, and he said to himself, she can even come after me here, she and her money, she can even follow me into the fields and spoil my work.

"Luigi," she said, patiently. "You do not seem to understand. I have rented this farm for six months but it is necessary to fix it up. This will benefit you also. As soon as it is properly cleaned and painted I shall have a cook and you will be given your meals. So you will not have to trouble any more yourself. Also your room will be painted and clean and comfortable and that is better than living as you do. If you are unwilling to help in any way then at least give me permission to move your things. The painters cannot work."

Why does she want all the rooms anyhow? Luigi thought. She is alone. She needs only one room or at most two.

"I have work to do," he said.

She went back to the house. It was too hot; it was so hot your head hurt and anything made you angry. The smell from the kitchen infuriated her. I do not understand dirt, she thought, and despise all people who accept it. And the flies.

"I will move Luigi's possessions," she said to the painter, "since he is unwilling."

The mason arrived and looked at the kitchen drains.

5

The Heart of Another

Why ever did the woman take this house, he wondered. She could get a clean apartment in town where there were other people to talk to and the market close by; anything would be better than this pigsty. He did not care about mountains and mimosa trees were nothing to him and silence was merely unpleasant. However, the woman was American; you could never tell about Americans. He frowned at the drains, discussed at great length the insuperable difficulties of the work, and charged her three times the proper wages.

The painter called to her and said, "Madame, it will take two coats of oil. I had not imagined the work. That will cost more." He was sorry for her. It would take two coats of oil, but it was not worth it. What did she want with the place anyhow? Had she perhaps a sorrow or had she done a crime? It did not seem reasonable.

"All right," the woman said. "Whatever you like."

"It is not what I like," he said stiffly. "It is the condition of the walls."

"All right, all right."

She went under the trees and began making lists: screening, kitchen utensils, garden chairs, electric-light bulbs, icebox. God, she thought, I'll have to go to Bastia to get all this junk. And the money. Stop it, she told herself; you wanted a home, then you have to make one. She had somehow imagined that you wanted a home and there it was, with mountains to the left and all,

6

whereas this was like a railway station with people rushing in and out, asking for more money, wanting orders
and explanations, and the sun flattening you out, blinding and choking you.

The painter met her seriously at the farm gate and
said, "Madame, Luigi is a saboteur."

"A what?"

"He slept in the large bedroom last night. He moved
the bed so that it has rubbed paint off the wall and he
upset a pail of varnish. Now I will have to buy more and
also scrape the floor."

Luigi was working in the farthest field.

"Why didn't you sleep in your room?" she said when
she had found him.

"It is too crowded and too hot."

"Then fix it. Go and fix it immediately."

"No."

"This cannot go on, Luigi."

He turned to her, he had not stopped working, bending down to break the earth around the vines. "You understand nothing," he said. "You know nothing about the
land. I must work all day and all tomorrow and until the
harvest. The house is nothing to me. It is the land."

Beyond her anger she kept thinking, he hates me and
he fears me and I want nothing that is his. But we must
have a home. To be safe in now and to remember later
no matter what happens. And Luigi cannot destroy that;
I will not allow it, not Luigi or any one.

7

She walked into town, hurrying and breathless, and found Signoret's lawyer.

"Luigi will have to take a room in the town," she said. "He will not let me get the house arranged. It is bad enough to have to do everything and it is very expensive. At least I will not argue it out with him every day."

The lawyer fluttered his hands and offered her a chair and told her in a voice like glue not to make herself bad blood over the whole thing, it was of course the heat, he could not regret it more but as she would be the first to see, her contract allowed for Luigi's presence, the vines could not be lost.

"He can live in town and work at the farm in the day. I will not have him in the house."

The lawyer would discuss the matter but did not think. . . . Even if he helped me, she told herself, I would not like that little man.

On the way back from Bastia the bus toppled and swayed over the roads and the Corsicans howled to each other in that language which combines the worst features of both French and Italian; and the two days shopping in Bastia had been exhausting, boring, and expensive. But that is all over, she thought, all the worst is over.

The house would be ready and he would come from the hospital in Spain, with his wound healed or almost healed and the months of fighting behind him, and he would find their home white and fresh with the dark green fringe of the eucalyptus trees around it. She would lead him through the rooms and watch his face for the pleasure in it. There would be flowers in the square raftered living room and a moderate fire in the brick fireplace and upstairs he would laugh at the huge tub, like a lidless coffin built of bright tiles. At the end of the afternoon there would be cool things to drink under the mimosa trees and at night they would read in comfortable chairs with good lamps beside them. It would be very quiet; she would make the place lovely and safe for them, for whatever time remained.

The house was better: four rooms were white and now that they were clean you saw how comforting the old rafters were, how good the fireplaces, and the red-tiled floors were pleasant and simple beneath the new walls. The smell of paint made the house fresh and it was cooler. She told herself that she had been right all along.

The painter caught up with her on the road. She stood between the walls, in the shade, smiling to herself because she liked this narrow dusty track leading from her farm to the sea.

"Madame," he said and puffed a little since it was still summer and he was not used to running, "I must warn you about Luigi."

"What now?"

"I do not know whether it is true but word has gone

9

about that you are going to send him away from the land. He has talked about it in the Deux Amis, the last two nights."

"Yes?"

"And you know," said the painter, "any man who lives alone for eleven years, with no one to talk to except the grapes, is mad. Evidently."

"I am not going to send him away from anything," she said wearily. "If he dislikes the house then he must take a room in the town. That is all."

"Naturally," the painter said. "It is to his advantage but he does not understand."

Luigi clearly did not understand. He stood before the door of his small dirty room with his arms outstretched and faced her and the painter looked on, as astonished as she was and as shocked. Luigi said no one was going to enter his room, no one was going to paint it; it was his room and he would keep it and no one would make him go away and no one would take the land from him. He talked in Italian and French and cursed her and then he stood there with tears running down his face and said over and over until his voice failed, "What is it to you? But to me it is my whole life, my whole life."

She tried to explain to him but he would not listen. He had gone through it all in his own mind, slowly, working in the sun. He knew now that she wanted him to go away; he would lose his year's work and more than that. Where could he go? Not to Italy again ever and in

France there was no work for a man. This was his place
and it was the last place he could find. He had made the
vines grow, he knew them all, and this piece of earth between the mountains and the sea was the only home he
could imagine. There was no family to take him in; he
was a stranger here and had no friends, only people who
spoke to him briefly in the café on the nights when he
went looking for company in town. But why did she
want this, how had he harmed her? She must be a wicked
and cruel woman who desired a man to suffer, without
reason. He would not let her come into his room anyhow; he would keep that until the last, until she sent the
police to drive him away from where he lived.

"Luigi, it is only to make it clean and pleasant for
you," she said. "But if you like it the way it is——"

He understood. She would have the room painted and
she would put her furniture into it. And then it would
be hers and she would say: I want my room, you can go.

"No," he said, his voice rising. "No, no."

The painter followed her down the road. He was a
kind and sensible man and he wished to comfort her.
She ought to have a husband, he thought, who would fix
it up with Luigi or else hit him. Women are all alike, he
decided, even if they are rich and American and go
about the world giving orders and doing things for themselves. Women are always in trouble, the same everywhere.

11

"Luigi is not a bad man," he said, "just stupid."

"Yes."

"If you would give me the pleasure of having a drink," the painter said, "before lunch. It will be cool and a change for the ideas."

"Thank you."

She walked very fast in the sun. The painter was a big man but heavy and he wished she would not race along this way. Take things easier, he thought, they all straighten out in the end.

They turned off the narrow farm road into the highway, walking past the pines that grew behind the beach. There was a little wind now from the sea and she walked more slowly.

"I do not understand him," the woman said, at last. "That is the trouble. If I knew what was the matter, I could talk to him."

"He is just stupid," the painter said, "but he will be all right later."

"I want to make a lovely place," she said. "I cannot see why he hates that so. It would be good for him too."

"He does not understand."

"I never had a home," she said, "and it must be ready. My husband is coming from the hospital in Spain."

"Oh," the painter said, thinking, well that is fine; it makes some sense now.

"And who knows how much time there is?" she said,

talking for herself. "It is not as if there were ten years or twenty years. It is in months now. I want to be happy," she said, standing still in the road and looking at the painter, feeling she had to tell some one. It was not just foolishness, this house and all the effort; she was not a rich woman with a light whim for Corsican farms. "I want us to be happy in our own house, for whatever peace remains."

"The war?" the painter said.

"Yes."

"I will be mobilized the fourth day," the painter said. "But you are a woman and a foreigner; it will change nothing for you."

"It will change everything, for me and all the world."

"I am an anti-Fascist," the painter said, "and if they attack us, we must fight and win."

"Yes," she said, "but it need never have come to this; it can still be stopped. And in war, it is mostly the good people who die. And afterward it is probably much the same as it was before."

"You are a defeatist," he said, with grave disapproval.

"No," she said, and smiled at him, "I am an anti-Fascist too, only I am tired and I know many good people who are dead."

Where had she come from after all, he wondered, and who was she? He had only thought she was a rich woman who wanted her house painted: not a bad woman but not interesting, just some one to pay for the paint.

13

"In Spain," she went on. "They have also died in other countries but I know it best in Spain."

He took her hand and began to shake it warmly, saying "Well, good, now that is good," over and over, delighted and surprised. So she had been to Spain and was an anti-Fascist and her man must have fought with the Internationals and been wounded since he was returning from a Spanish hospital. That was a different matter; that made it something else again. He would get her house fixed and tell Luigi to behave himself and before that they would have a drink like friends and comrades.

They passed the garage and the painter called to the garagiste, "Come and have a glass, Jean Michel, with an anti-Fascist comrade." Jean Michel came out of the garage, wiping oil from his hands, looked at the woman, said "with pleasure" and joined them at a table in the café.

Well, she thought, I may have troubles but I have certainly got pals. They drank *pastis,* drinking to Spain and to America and to France and to Democracy until at last she felt her weariness and haste falling from her, the problem of Luigi dwindling into a prickly but not serious nuisance, and she looked across the long curving blond beach to the red rock mountains and found Corsica a fine place after all and she at home in it.

The painter introduced her to a carpenter who made sturdy bookshelves and tables. He took her to a seamstress who worked rapidly and well and fixed covers for the chairs and beds. The electrician appeared miraculously the day he said he would and put plugs in the walls and arranged the Frigidaire. Two men were hired by the painter and in a few days they had cleaned the garden and the ground around the house, hauling away the empty wine bottles and tin cans of Luigi's long dirty tenancy, bringing the flowers to life, cutting and watering the grass. The painter came one day with a silent energetic middle-aged woman who had a gray permanent and a clean white dress and she was installed as cook. It seemed to happen easily and the woman did not notice the heavy airlessness behind her eucalyptus trees. It was all coming true as she had planned.

The painter did everything except paint Luigi's room for Luigi was determined and at last they decided to leave him in the small hot room crammed with the shabby suitcases, the odds and ends of old paper, broken tools, rags, chipped glasses and medicine bottles that he apparently cherished. There were newly painted chairs for his room, tables, a blue bed cover, fresh linen, and a mirror, but he would not accept these things and they agreed not to worry with him. If he wanted to be so stupid, let him.

She had been at home now for three days. When she woke in the morning she would lie in her room and listen to the flies buzzing beyond her glittering screens, the small wind that rustled the fern leaves of the mimosas and perhaps, far off, Thérèse moving in the kitchen. She lay on her back and admired the white sun-bright ceiling. Then she would make the pillows comfortable behind her and sitting up, enjoy the sight of the new wood bookshelves and the deep, pale yellow chairs. When she rang Thérèse came to her with a breakfast tray, pottery jars of honey and jam, fresh butter smoothed into a small saucer, the little pots for coffee and hot milk and she and Thérèse spoke together seriously and respectfully of the day's meals as if they had both lived here a long time and had between them for years back and for years to come the managing of this thick-walled house. She would walk about her house in the morning, opening the linen closet for the joy of seeing the sheets piled so stiff and white together, the knubbly heaps of bath towels, the flat squares of the table napkins. She would stand in the living room, with new flowers in her hands, admiring her work and wondering how she had lived before with no house to tend and watch over. She read in the sun, turning the pages without remembering them, grateful for the warmth and the slowness of time. The world was someplace far away. Only the S.S. *Ile de Beauté* led to it on Tuesdays and Thursdays across the flat sea to Nice. She was safe. And soon this would be a home for two people, a real place. The weather was so lovely that you could not believe anything bad would happen ever.

The painter came to have an aperitif at six o'clock when the sun lay behind the eucalyptus trees and the mountains and the sky turned from gold to pale green. He was as proud of the house as she was; it was, he thought, the finest house around here and he was glad to have a share in it.

He let himself down carefully into a striped deck chair under the trees and remarked, "These are fine chairs. Did you order them from Nice?"

"No. From Bastia."

"They were very costly?"

"No. The end of the season. Only seventy francs."

"Ah."

So they had also the comfortable thing of ownership and ways and means and he thought that despite her independence and her restlessness and knowing too much and thinking all the time, she would still make a good wife; at least she could fix a house and run it comfortably and a man would always be pleased with that.

"The priest at Calenzana is dead," he said, and cooled his hands with his glass.

"So?"

"Yes. The women there are poor superstitious things, very ignorant and superstitious."

"I do not know Calenzana."

"The women say that when the priest died a great flame came out of his mouth." He waited to see whether she would believe this. He was a socialist himself and did not believe such stories but all the women in Calvi believed it and Jean Michel himself who, though a socialist, was also pious was not prepared to deny it.

"I do not see how that is possible," she said.

"I told them the same," the painter said, relieved. "You can see how hard it is to form a socialist bloc in a place where people believe such things."

Luigi walked up the path from the vines, holding two spades in his hands. The painter greeted him but Luigi did not answer. He threw the spades down on the grass and walked away.

"He does not put his spades in the tool room?" the painter asked.

"No. He does what he can to make a disorder here."

"He looks very strange," the painter said, "around the eyes."

"We do not speak any more. I sent Thérèse to him yesterday to ask whether she could clean his room but he told her that if ever she entered his room he would strike her."

"He drinks," the painter said. "I cannot understand him. He was never a bad man, just simple or stupid, but now he comes into the town every night and drinks with the Algerian who sells rugs. Sometimes he talks wildly."

"It is a pity," she said, "but what can I do?"

He shrugged his shoulders; there was nothing to do and yet he felt badly that a worker should behave in this manner. It was stupid and it prejudiced people. He had tried to reason with Luigi one night at the Deux Amis but Luigi had screamed at him that he got money from the woman, the way every one did; they were all crooks

and liars and only cared for money and he Luigi knew
what he could expect. The land was his, he had shouted,
and he would keep it. There was no use telling him anything because he would not listen.

The painter did not speak to the woman of this because
it would only worry her and at last he said he would have
to go home as his wife did not like to spoil the supper
waiting for him. She walked a little way down the road
with him and he said he would come out some afternoon next week and put a coat of green paint on the gate
which was faded and many thanks for the aperitif and
Salut.

Thérèse brought the matter up, the next morning. She
was timid about it because she did not like to bear tales or
make trouble. But she did not want to be blamed herself.

"There is something disagreeable, Madame," she began.

"Yes."

"About Luigi."

"Tell me."

"I wish I could clean his room," Thérèse said, though
this was a digression. "It is not a nice thing to have a
room like that over my kitchen. The kitchen as Madame
knows is as clean as a pin and you can look anywhere in
it, at any time, and find it always so. But his room is nothing but filth and there is an odor." She stopped because
these were ugly things to talk about.

"Well, only that, there is this odor. It is unpleasant to
have such a thing coming into my kitchen."

"I will speak to Luigi," but a lot of good it will do, she thought.

"There is something else. I only mention it because I do not wish Madame to think it was me. Last night Luigi broke the glass pitcher and the four glasses, the ones for iced tea. He must have done this late, when he came home, for I found them broken in the morning when I arrived."

Well, she thought, I will now have to take a stand. But why is he like this? And why does he have to spoil the morning and why does he have to walk about the farm with his face ugly and angered, and why won't he let his room be made clean and comfortable for him? She thought, pretty soon I will hate him too and be as stupid as he is.

At lunch time she called Luigi to her. He came unwillingly and she stood on the doorstep looking at him, feeling absurd to treat a grown man in this way.

"I understand you broke some things in the kitchen last night."

"Yes," he said.

"It was an accident of course."

It had not been an accident but he could not think quickly what to say. He had done it purposely, slowly, breaking first the pitcher and then each glass, one by one, throwing them into the stone sink but not with force; he did not want to waken her. He had been drinking, it was true, but this had nothing to do with it. He broke them to show her how he hated her and the fine things in her

20

house. All evening he had been talking with the Algerian who was his friend, telling him over and over how Signoret signed the contract with the woman and how the farm was no longer his; he was only a visitor. He could not do this and he could not do that, he could not go into the rooms, he was supposed to put his tools away, he must come for meals when he was called.

And he could not sleep, a dog could not sleep in that small room under the roof with the closed windows. He woke uneasily with his head hurting, and looked at that crowded hot room and every morning it came over him again, the injustice of it, and how they had done this to him and were all against him. The painter was against him and even Madame Morelli, who ran the Deux Amis and knew everything, said he was not reasonable. They were waiting until they could find an excuse to put him out. And they acted as if he had some disease, they drew away from him. The cook would not take her meals with him but gave him his food first and sat down to eat only when he had gone.

He was only an Italian, he said to himself, a poor man who could not read and all he knew about was the vines. But he had lived here for eleven years and things had been plain and understandable and he never had trouble with any one. Now there was nothing but trouble and people wishing him evil, wishing to take away his home and his land, his work and his chance to live. She has not the right, he thought, and now she will have me arrested for destroying her property. Dimly, twisting his hands and looking beyond her into the house, he tried to see where this had all started, where it had come from and what had made it like this, until it was bigger than he was and he was just a man who did things he had not planned, in terror and hate but helplessly.

"Luigi," she said, half way between pity and sharpness, "what is the matter with you?"

With him, always with him, he was always the one they blamed. No one said anything about her; she had a right to go wherever she wished and destroy anything she saw and what he did was wrong and they were all against him.

"I broke them," he shouted, "I broke them. I cannot work and I cannot sleep and you are getting ready to take the land away from me too. But you cannot arrest me and put me in jail. I know you would like to see me in prison," he said, craftily, "so you could be alone here and have my room for the cook and not have to feed me. I know you would like that. But they will not catch me."

He passed his hand over his eyes and pushed his hair back from his forehead. He seemed uncertain himself of what he had said, and bewildered. She was staring at him now, saying to herself, he is more than stupid. He is mad. He must be. She thought, for weeks that small stupid brain has been working this thing over and over and found no answer and now it is beyond him; he has nothing left to think with. Or can it be the heat? she thought; it is possible he has a sunstroke, a fever, and he does not know what he is saying. But his eyes frightened her.

He turned and ran for the gate, awkwardly and unsteadily, as if the sun had blinded him. He did not look back.

She did not speak to Thérèse of this but only said, "We will not worry about Luigi; you can serve lunch."

The farm itself seemed quieter. She had always waited, without thinking, to hear him stamp up from the vines and fling his tools onto the grass; she had waited to hear him mumbling in the tool shed, purposely rattling the old rusty iron spades, scythes, and pruning knives. You could always feel his enmity through the walls even if you ignored him. It was better without him and she hoped he would stay away. But as the afternoon went on she found she could not read and she kept remembering his eyes.

I will not be silly about it, she decided, but she went back to the house and wrote a note to the painter: "I am unquiet for Luigi, who talked strangely this morning and left the house. Would you be so good as to watch him and let me know where he is." She asked Thérèse to take the note into town and when Thérèse had gone, the quiet of the farm was like night.

Thérèse did not understand all this going and coming but she was worried. She returned with a message from the painter.

"He says to tell Madame that he has not seen Luigi all day, so perhaps Luigi has gone to Ile Rousse or Saint Florent to look for other work. He says for Madame not to alarm herself and he will let her know if Luigi returns. . . . There is trouble, Madame?"

Why didn't he write it to me, the woman thought; now the whole village will know.

"No," she said, "nothing. You need not wait dinner for Luigi either, Thérèse."

Thérèse served dinner half an hour early. She wanted to get home before it was really dark; she did not want to meet Luigi on the narrow track between the shadowy walls when the sky was already black. You could not trust those solitary men; they were always strange and she had heard of Luigi's drinking. She washed the dishes rapidly and came to see the woman before she left, trying to act as if this early hour was usual and saying as always at night, "Is there anything Madame wishes from the town?"

"No," the woman said. "Thank you and good night." But she knew why Thérèse was leaving and she wished that she could go too or ask Thérèse to stay and she thought, I will not make a fool of myself but when you stop to think about it perhaps it is not too wise to live alone, far from any one or the town, without a gun, without anything just in case.

She locked all the doors, put out the lights, and went upstairs. She stood beside the door of her bedroom for some time and at last turned the large stiff key in the lock. Second line of defense, she mocked herself, what a state you are in, my poor shivering creature. It's the quiet, she told herself.

It was the quiet and the darkness, too. You could not see the first row of vines, from the window. The land lay about her without shape or marking, just a blackness that shut her tight inside her house. The town was five kilometers away and there were no neighbor's lights to make the land friendly. You could not tell where the sky began. It looks smoky, she thought; no it doesn't, it just looks black.

The reading lamp lighted her pillow and glowed over the bed. Beyond the foot of the bed the blackness started; the windows were only a shining in the dark. I wish they locked, she thought, and then she said to herself coldly, aloud: "What is the matter with you?" Her voice was very frightening in the shadowy room. Better not try that again, she decided, and suddenly she wanted to laugh.

Now read, she told herself. Go on, read. You didn't hear anything. There is no one here except you. From the gate to the house, no one; from the well to the farthest row of eucalyptus, no one; from the wall by the road to the kitchen garden, no one. So stop it. Either read or go to sleep.

She turned out the reading light. There was nothing to hear at all. The room seemed very close but that was silly, it was exactly like all other nights. Well, what can he do? she said to herself, he can either come home or not come home. He can't do anything. People never really do anything. Corsica is France; they have laws, they have jails. You better be careful or you'll get just as queer as he is. Islands, she thought, terrible places, and went to sleep.

She did not know what sound awakened her or what time it was. The blackness lay over everything as before and only a faint shining in the wall showed her where the windows were. She was awake but it was not true about how you waked and everything was clear and you were in possession of all your wits. She felt heavy and blind and her mind was no use to her. She had heard something, but what and from what direction? Then she heard it again, the handle of the door turning, and she was afraid. She thought: be very very very quiet, he is mad anyhow and if he does not hear you maybe he will think you are gone or dead and maybe he will not try. . . . Or should she get up and stand near the door and speak to him in a false commanding voice, threatening him with punishment and ordering him away? I cannot move, she thought, it's too dark, and if he is all the way mad, what must his face look like now. She remembered the sly wild eyes and her mouth was dry and her throat tight and pounding.

He might have been talking to himself or whispering to her through the door or just breathing. There was a noise anyhow, something, and the handle kept turning slowly, slowly from left to right, though she could not see it but only hear it. She had pulled herself up against the head-

26

board of the bed and sat there, shivering but quiet, and waited. Then she began to think, jerkily at first, about real things. Would the door hold if he tried to break it in, that was the first point. Yes, or anyhow probably. Now then, now then. Try to think about it straight. I couldn't do anything against him, she thought; I have no gun and I am not strong enough. How can I get out of here? That door, she told herself, that door where he is, or the windows? From the window to the ground, twelve feet, fifteen feet, something—anyhow too much to jump and be sure of landing safely. And then afterward, what would you do? Run. Run where? Run down the road to town. Five kilometers. Any man can run faster than any woman. Don't be a fool. Run through the vines to the eucalyptus, hope to lose him there, somewhere. He has lived here eleven years, he knows every weed in the grass. Don't be a fool. Then what, she thought wildly—I have to do something, there must be something.

Then the door handle was quiet and the breathing or the whispering stopped. You wouldn't have thought that would be worse, she said to herself. What frightened her now, beyond everything else, was the thought of his face. How could it be, how was a man's face if he had gone all the way mad? People did not come at night quietly, only breathing or whispering, slowly and slyly turning a door handle, unless they were mad. So how would it be? The eyes she could guess, but the mouth and the hair on the forehead, the way the head itself sat on the neck? How

27

would a man look who came in the night this way and without a reason except his madness? What am I to do now? she thought. He can be coming from anywhere, now there's no noise. He can be doing anything.

For a time after it started she was not sure what it was but she thought that if she moved from the bed there would be the empty room around her and here anyhow she had the wall at her back. He couldn't do that, he couldn't do that. The windows shone in the darkness, without locks. He must have taken the garden table; he would be standing on that now, that would be the squeaking sound, the legs of the table bending under him; yes, so he must be standing on that and trying to get a hand hold on the balcony rails and if he could he would swing himself up, until he got over the railing and stood on the narrow cement balcony. And then there were the windows, without any locks at all.

There was only the small distant noise of wood, like steps cracking under sudden weight. She saw it clearly: he would be standing on the table but his arms would be short of the railings, maybe three or four or five feet short, and he would reach first and then he would try to jump for them knowing that if once his hands fastened on them he could pull himself up. But he could not get his hands on them; when he jumped the table shook and sagged and he could not touch the railing. He tried and tried and she heard his breath coming out of him (or did she think she heard it?) and she could see his hands, bigger than hands could ever be, hooked and curved to grasp the railings where they joined the cement floor of the balcony.

She heard, very clearly, how he jumped down from the table and how he dragged it away under the trees where it had stood before and then she could hear nothing.

She pushed far back against the headboard of the bed and pulled the covers up to her chin. She felt stiff and aching with cold. She made herself smaller and smaller in the bed and quieter. Now she was waiting for him to figure it out: the chair on top of the table, if the table is not high enough, get a chair from the kitchen. It's like being buried, she thought: you can't hear and no one can hear you.

There was the little clock on the table by the bed but she would have to turn on a light or strike a match to see it. I can't do that, I can't change anything. Let it just go on as it is, wait, wait. And time did not matter anyhow; there was only night and day. As long as it was night, he could try again.

She tried to think where he could be and what he could be doing in this silence. But her mind would make no picture of him, he could be doing nothing orderly or reasonable, nothing you could imagine. He would not be in the kitchen, eating or drinking. He would not be walking down the road away from the house, to escape from what he had wanted to do. He would not be in his room, packing or asleep, or sitting on a chair waiting for the night to

29

pass. He could do none of these things, not after the turning door handle and the table beneath the balcony.

It will be daylight soon, she said to herself; it will be daylight soon. The cold held her and weakened her. The silence spread through the room and through the house and outside; in the windless before-dawn, the trees were quiet. Slowly, lying still and listening, her body loosened and her fear blurred into a thick numb weariness and when the sky lightened to a milky gray, she slept.

When she woke she had slid sideways in the bed and one hand touched the tiles of the floor. She pulled herself straight and saw through the windows the pale clean early morning sky. For a time she lay there and tried to remember back through the night. Her room was bright and tidy and not suitable for nightmares. The branch of the pine tree moved like a plume in the small new wind and beyond her room the house was silent and friendly as on other mornings.

He must have been drunk, she thought, but I'm not going through any more nights like that. Drunk is one thing and creeping around the house terrifying people is another thing. She was angry with her fear and with the memory of that waiting in the dark. I'm not going to be terrorized in my own house, it's too absurd. I won't have it. It's enough now; now he'll really have to go. I won't even speak to him, she thought; I'll find Signoret and tell him that either I will give up the house or Luigi will

have to leave. I have a right to, she said to herself, after a
night like that. But she would not leave, not really; not
after making the place so fresh and lovely. It's my home,
she thought, you don't leave your home because a drunk
Italian crawls around scaring you in the night. He can live
in town until he gets sensible.

She went to the cupboard in the wall and found her
clothes: a sweater, tennis shoes, a pair of slacks. It was
almost seven. I'll walk into town right away, she decided,
and telephone Signoret. I don't even want to see Luigi, I
won't talk to him. He's got to get out immediately, this
morning, now.

She unlocked her door remembering how she had
watched it in the night, how she had feared for the
strength of the lock and the thickness of the wood. She
walked down the stairs past the dark corner where she
had thought Luigi might be waiting for her in the night
if she tried to run from her own home. A white and green
striped garden parasol stood in the corner, as reasonable
as daylight. It surprised her to find the door locked until
she remembered that Luigi had no key to this door, only
to the door of his own room. So he had come in that way,
by the outside steps that led from the garden directly up
to his room in the corner of the second floor. The key
was heavy and rusty and turned slowly in the lock. There
was no smell of coffee in the hall because it was too early
for Therèse, but she saw the day stretching ahead like
other days: the smell of coffee, the sound of a broom

31

sweeping the hall and the living room, the clatter of plates as Thérèse set the luncheon table under the mimosas, the rustling of the eucalyptus trees.

The screen door whined open on its hinges.

The garden lay fresh in the new sun. Sun glittered on the water in the bird bath, the dark red roses hung heavy with dew and the mimosa trees were fine as smoke against the sky. The vines grew in even rows, like little twisted fountains. The mountains were pink in the morning light and she could smell the sea.

She held the screen open and let the wind cool her face and the night fell away as something childish and unreal that had nothing to do with her.

She was in no hurry any more and she leaned against the arch of the doorway, feeling the rough sun-baked stone at her back. Her house and her land seemed finer than all other places. We are going to be very happy here, she thought. Then she remembered Luigi but without rancor. They had been silly all along, she decided, and last night the silliest of all but she would get it straightened out; there was no need to behave like an idiot and no doubt Luigi was ashamed of the whole business by now.

She turned contentedly to survey her property and saw the garden wall making a corner with the house. It was a pleasant corner, green and vine-covered, and the outside steps, faded with rain and sun, led up against this wall to Luigi's room on the second floor.

She stood still, her hand pressing on the stone doorway.

If you saw the steps and rope knotted to the railing at the top, you had to see it. It was an old short piece of rope that was no good for anything. . . . "Why don't you throw it away, Luigi?" "No," he said. "It is mine." Down, not far, but just a little way, he hung against the wall of the house. Hanging there with his head sideways, he seemed even smaller than she had remembered: small, brown and shabby. He wore only socks on his feet. They were coarse tan socks and too large for him and they puckered loosely over his toes. His hair looked very flat and had slanted across his forehead and on his left hand, on the little finger, he wore a large cheap ring with a red stone that she had never noticed before.

He tried the door and he climbed on the garden table and then he did that, in the dark, she thought. It didn't make any noise at all when he did it and he must have been very careful or else the rope would have broken. It was only an old piece of rope frayed at both ends; it was not good for anything.

She could think of nothing to do now, and nowhere to go. She would have to find some one and then they would come and take him down. It was a long way from the house to the gate and she walked slowly because she was tired. I only meant to make a home, she thought, I only meant to make a home. I only wanted the house to be lovely. She did not look back and she knew it was not her house and never would be. It was Luigi's house. It was Luigi's house now.

Night Before Easter

THE MAN from Chicago announced that it was his birth-day.

"Que?" said the man sitting next to me. *"Que dice?"*

"Su santo," I said. "His saint's day." I am not sure whether this means birthday in Spanish, or whether it has something to do with your first name and the saint after whom you are named and for all I know *"su santo"* would mean: it is the birthday of his saint.

"Thirty-nine," the man from Chicago said, and giggled. "Old. Finished."

"Felicitations," said the taxi driver. "Let us drink."

We raised our glasses. We were all drinking whiskey-and-soda, except Félix, who, was drinking coca-cola be-cause he thought he might have to play at the Fronton to-morrow night. He could see we were started on a long evening and he was taking care of himself.

The Basque whom I had never seen before, who looked like Caruso except with light hair and a kind jolly un-spoiled expression, began to sing like Caruso too. It was

34

a very imposing voice and Pachi who weaves the pelota baskets, sitting next to Caruso, pulled his chair closer and got in on the song. The taxi driver has a voice like a bull and Félix, who knows all the tunes and most of the words but hasn't much voice, sang too. It was two o'clock in the morning and there were still many people on the streets but the café was emptying. The singing attracted people from the outside and as the café is open to the street on three sides, we got a good crowd. Five colored boys stood on the pavement near our table and applauded or whistled if they did not care for the song and called out the names of songs they would like to hear sung and in between songs the Basques would say to them, "*qué va,* we are singing our own songs, go, leave us."

Two strangers came to our table. One had a bad eye that looked as if it had been boiled, it was larger than the other one and milky and unmoving. He put his arms around Félix's shoulders and said, "Thou knowest that I love thee like a son," and Félix laughed and said, "Sit down and be tranquil and have a drink."

"Do you know him, Félix?" I asked.

"I see him here sometimes."

"He seems to love you greatly."

"A poor crazy," Félix said.

The other man was apparently an old friend of theirs. He looked as if he worked in a garage.

"Who is he?" I asked. "Why don't you give him a drink?"

The light-haired Caruso called for a drink.

"Who is he?" I said.

"He is a man from Asturias," Pachi said, as if that would explain everything.

They went on singing.

"Come, come, come, my dearest, come, come, that I adore thee. . . ." It is gay music and sounds like a boating song. The colored boys thought it was fine. Then we sang the Basque hymn which is great music and when you sing it, or hear it sung, you wear a respectful face no matter how drunk you may be. It is a straight-rising, solid, brave and tragic song and they always sing it with pride and in mourning. To hear it makes you want to cry and it makes shivers go up and down your back and you can easily see how people who invented a song like that and sing it so beautifully would love their land.

The two waiters who were hanging around, wondering when we would leave but not being cross or hurried, sat down at the next table and said, *"Olé, Olé,"* after the Basque hymn.

"This is a fine birthday party," I said to the man from Chicago.

"I wish I were Spanish," he said.

"I can see how you feel."

He got up and came over and asked the man sitting next to me to lend him his chair.

"I want to talk to you," he said. His name was Walter

Thomas. I had met him at the Fronton, the last time he was in Habana. Pachi introduced him, saying, "A compatriot of thine, a great business man in vegetables." It seems he came to Cuba to buy pineapples or tomatoes or perhaps it was some other fruit or vegetable. He had known these Basques when they played pelota in Chicago at the Rainbow Gardens and they were often at his house, cooking Basque food, drinking wine and singing. I had never really talked to him but he was a good friend to the Basques, who were wonderful people, and he loved pelota and he was always pleasant and good-humored, drunk or sober, and he was shy.

"Look at these boys," he said. "They've never tried to live. They've never tried to do anything. And they've had fuller lives, not doing anything about it, than I have and I've been trying everything my whole life."

This was news to me. I thought he was a businessman who happened to be crazy about pelota.

He made a list for me of the things he had done: he had played a banjo in vaudeville and worked in the oil fields, he had been a common seaman and taught school, he had travelled everywhere, he had made and lost quite a good piece of money several times (which I am told is a very enlightening experience). Now he was thirty-nine and looking at the Basques he knew they were wiser, better off and sounder than he was, though they came from small villages in a country that was lost to them, spent their lives playing pelota or helping people play pelota, read only the Cuban newspapers and seemed to make no effort about living.

"Well," I said, helplessly. A birthday will make any one gloomy, a birthday is a time of accounting. You cannot escape it, and if you are a little drunk it is usually worse because you see things clearly and your pride is alcoholized so that you do not lie either to yourself or to other people.

"Well," I said. "They're very remarkable, of course."

"What have you got that I haven't got?" he said. "That's what I want to know. I want to talk to you a long time quietly, and find out. I want to know. I've done everything you have. I've been around. What is it anyhow? I'd like to sit under a tree somewhere and talk all day."

I did not want to get into any sad, comparative conversation; I did not want to waste a good evening making tipsy generalizations. I wanted to sing when I could catch the tune, or listen, or talk to Félix, who is not very clever but always tells me things that are interesting and that I am glad to learn. Besides that, Félix's face moves me and it is a pleasure to talk to him, to watch his mouth and to watch his smile.

"You're a fine man, Walter," I said. "Everybody thinks so. You don't have to worry about yourself."

Félix called across the table to the one who looked like Caruso. *"Angel,"* he said. "Sing 'All the Negroes drink coffee.'"

"Is his name really Angel?" I asked.

Félix said, puzzled, "Why? Certainly."

"It's a pretty name," I said.

Angel said, "It is three o'clock and when I go home I will receive some words."

"Who from?" I asked.

"My mother-in-law," he said, and shook his head. "A rare woman."

The one who weaves pelota baskets said to me, in English, "Hees mother law very tough, mean, strong old woman. I go his house, she chase me out."

"If you will be punished anyhow," Félix said, "why not stay out all night? It is so late now that the punishment will be the same."

"*Pues,*" said Angel, "you speak the truth. Let us sing."

"He has a marvellous voice," I said.

"That man is paid to sing," Félix said with admiration. "He makes money, singing. That is something intelligent. You can sing until you are old. It is not like pelota. He has an agreeable, easy work and he is as good now as he was ten years ago."

"I know a lot of songs but they're no good," Walter Thomas said.

"Me, too."

"What I mean is," he went on, "I've done a lot and I know a lot and it doesn't show. I'm just like everybody else. I'm ordinary. And here are these boys and even you. I can't figure it out."

I saw he was worried and unhappy about himself but I

39

loved this café because it was friendly, no one ever hurried you to pay, the food was fine, they put the whiskey bottle on the table and left it and charged you for whatever you said you drank, it was like a café in Spain too, and being here with Spaniards, singing (and now they were singing the songs that the Basques sang in the war) was all so good and satisfying and pleasant that I did not want to get involved in Walter Thomas' troubles. He was a nice man but he seemed like anybody else to me too, and daily troubles are the business of the people who have them. Outside it was warm and with a blurred moon, already summer, and earlier that evening we had seen the finest pelota game I have seen thus far, which became so exciting you held yourself stiff and did not breathe easily and you could feel the minutes and as the ball swung and cracked against the wall you felt the movement of the players' bodies in your body and heard the crack of the ball all through your head. It had already been a fine night and it was not yet ended.

"You're okay," I said a little impatiently. "You're all right."

"What passes with him?" Félix asked me. He was sitting on the other side.

"Don't leave me," I said. "He is sad and wants to talk and I do not want to talk. So don't go away in any case."

"Let us go to a cabaret and dance," said Pachi. He is perhaps the happiest one of all; every day he must wake up and think with joy of all the delightful things he can do that day, though he has no money to mention. He knows every one in Habana and is friends with every one and likes to do everything.

There were only five of us in the taxi, the others had somehow gotten lost between the table and the street. Angel was still singing.

The night club was an open patio; some tables were placed against the inside walls but most of them were under the sky, as was the dance floor, and the cement sides of the buildings which lined the patio looked like the flat white walls of houses in Tunis, with the moon on them. The floor show was going on. A stout but agile Negress wearing a stylized rhumba costume of lavender ruffles stood up in front of the orchestra with her bottom towards the audience and she circled her bottom from left to right, around, up, down, shaking it once at the end of a complete circle, while the drummer clashed his cymbals and her solid round smooth-moving buttocks somehow gave the impression of a mechanical thing, like a butter churner. The orchestra played loudly and the audience drank and talked and did not watch.

"She would sleep with you all night for two dollars," Walter Thomas observed morosely, as if this proved also how little there was in life, it was all within your grasp and when you had it you had nothing.

"Two dollars?" I said with wonder. She looked more expensive to me.

"What do you say?" Félix asked.

"Walter says you could get that dancer for two dollars."
"Why not?" Félix asked. "Her and many others and much more."

More Negresses, these thinner, a golden brown color, now pranced out wearing the same costume in yellow, the costume covering the breasts and making a long tail-like train behind, leaving the legs bare. They danced as they do here in the comparsas of the fiesta, three steps to the right and then the outward and upward jerk of the stomach, three steps to the left and the stomach rising with a quick sudden thrust, the head moving back at the same time. They propel themselves forward with sideways pulls of the elbows and it is a simple dance, danced to the beat of drums, which sometimes in the night streets of Habana during the carnival season can become very wild and chokingly exciting to watch. It is a dance that calls no attention to the face of the dancer but keeps your eyes fast to the strutting jerking body and finally you only notice the belly and legs. Only Negroes could do it so well and arrogantly and with so little shame. The people at the tables did not watch this either.

"Very boring," said Angel.

"A mediocre place," said the other Basque, the quiet one who has a business and goes to an office every day.

"We ought to go to the French Casino," Walter said.

I thought it was a wonderful place. The basket-weaver asked me to dance. He was very man-about-town, speaking to every one on the dance floor. We saw the great back of the Jai-Alai, the one who had played that night the winning inspired game and I stopped to tell him how good he had been. *"Regulár,"* he said, *"Regulár,"* with the proud self-confident lift of the shoulders which denies the modest word and states that he played like a wonder and knew it and that you would probably never know just how well he played. He was dancing with a tall, very thin, blondish girl with a dead face.

"Who is she?" I asked Pachi.

"A señorita," he said. "A señorita, *she* says. Now it is the fashion for the big pelotaris to go out with señoritas."

We came back to the table when the music stopped and Félix shouted across the crowded room to a table where three men were sitting.

"Olé," he called. "You speak only to your friends when they have money?"

The three laughed and waved to him.

"Very serious," Félix said, shaking his head. "No good tonight."

"If you play tomorrow, oughtn't you to get some sleep?"

"No. Want to dance?"

We passed the other great pelota player, the one who had lost, sitting at a table with many people, not talking and looking at the floor.

"He is sad," I said.

"Qué va, sad. He is tired."

Félix dances as if he were afraid of what he would do if he really danced. It is all there but checked, so that he holds you loosely and you know how it would be if he held you close against him. The motion is kept in his body and you feel it thinly with his arm slack across your back. But it is a motion that you can guess at and one of the things I want to see is Félix, drunk and free, dancing with a woman he is not careful of. Félix is not married and he only deals with women, as is the custom, quickly at night for money or not for money according to necessity and not remembering it afterwards either gratefully or angrily, just not remembering it at all. If he marries there will be the special thing for his wife: but they have not been brought up to have a need or use for women, except the one who is the wife and the others for bed. They come to my house to play tennis on the days they are not going to play pelota and we have the war in Spain between us, the memory and the understanding of the war, and that makes me their friend. It is a unique position and they regard me as a phenomenon in their lives, for whom there are different rules.

So Félix danced with me as if he did not mean to be dancing.

Even that way he is better than most men and all the time he talked in the way he has, with a vague mocking melancholy, telling me how bad this life was, staying out all night, drinking, consorting with whores and other bad-livers, how when he was forty he would be a ruined old man, how it was very boring to go to such cabarets: and all the time you saw that he was a happy boy on the whole, with a great talent for his work, and ambition, and that he was still young enough to delight in his freedom, in having his own money and being able to stay up all night and sleep with whatever women he could afford.

I danced with Angel which was like riding in a rowboat on a choppy sea.

When we came back to the table, Walter Thomas was gone.

"Where is our American?"

The quiet Basque said, "He has probably gone to the French Casino. He has a friend there. It diverts him more. You understand?"

The respectability of the place began to depress Angel who, in a silence between dance numbers, suddenly started to sing. The others joined him and soon the remaining people in the cabaret had come to stand near us or turned to listen and the orchestra, seizing the chance, put their instruments in cases and cut off the light in the drum and prepared to go home.

A small silvery man, who was one of the betting agents at the Fronton, sang very well indeed and then left singing his good-bys. Angel undid his tie and collar and his neck swelled out and the songs grew louder and stronger, thrown back from the walls of the houses around the patio.

Suddenly Walter Thomas returned, walking with a slight wobble, and with him was a dark, not pretty, not

45

young, not well dressed, not even very clean woman who wore a small hat with a veil, two beauty spots, and an olive-green dress. He introduced her and I shook hands and Pachi made some quick joking remark in Spanish.

"Pachi says," the man from Chicago explained, "that he is very pleased to meet the lady. She costs all of five dollars and is worth meeting."

"Where did you find her?"

"Over there at the bar," he said. "I still want to talk to you. It isn't a question of money: I can make money. What is it then?"

What is what, I thought. It was after five o'clock. I wanted the Basques to go on singing. I felt very happy and flushed in the face and full of energy.

"You're sort of an ideal woman," Walter Thomas said. It was then that I noticed the dark lady holding his hand, firmly and possessively. She didn't want to lose him; it was too late to find any one else.

"I'm what?" I said. I was enchanted with how she had his hand.

"Like Myrna Loy," he said. "In that movie, 'The Thin Man.' That kind of woman. It's sort of an ideal."

"Look," Félix said, laughing, "the *puta* asked me what goes on. She said: is he with me or with her? I said, he's with you, stupid: so now she grabs him to make sure."

"He's certainly got himself fixed up, all right."

"He comes here for a vacation," Felix said. "If that is his taste."

46

"He's too drunk to know."

"Maybe he cannot see in this light. Maybe he thinks it is better than it is."

"Vamos," said Angel. "I go home to face my mother-in-law."

"We'll go to the French Casino," Walter Thomas said.

"I think I better go home," I said. "I'm not used to this high-life."

Félix paid. Félix always seems to pay.

We had now started towards the door and Walter Thomas had hold of my arm and the whore had hold of him. I wondered whether it was going to develop into a real pull.

"I've tried everything," he said. "I've worked at everything. I know all kinds of people. That's why I don't understand."

By now we were on the street and Angel was singing softly to himself and taxi drivers had clustered around us saying, "Wanna taxi, Mees. Wanna taxi, Meester," and I was saying: let's walk, I live close by here, and the man from Chicago was saying, let's go to the French Casino, don't leave me.

We left him though, standing on the pavement under a street lamp, the woman's arm through his, her body pressed determinedly against him and he looked surprised, lonely and a little afraid. He's going to try something more, I thought, and he still won't understand.

The Basques laughed at him standing there so unwilling but so caught and waved and we walked down the street.

I was staying at a hotel in town because they were painting my house and it was full of puzzled paint-stained men and it smelled awful.

At the door of the hotel, Angel said, *"Chicos,* what time is it?"

"Six minus fifteen," Félix said.

"Man, I must go to Mass," Angel said. "Hurry. There is no need to go home anyhow and the old woman will not have the opportunity to talk until after breakfast."

"Mass?" I said.

"I sing in the Easter Mass." Angel made a little gesture, rubbing his thumb against his other fingers, which means "money."

"Let us all go," Pachi said. "And listen to how beautifully Angel can sing."

"It is too late to go to bed," Félix said reasonably. "Besides it is fine music in church."

"Pues," said the quiet Basque, "you go, but I will go home."

"Why, man?" Pachi said. "Why leave us now? The music will be fine."

"It isn't that," the other said. "It is only that I have not been to Mass in twenty-six years."

"Well come, then," Félix said. "It cannot hurt you. It will not obligate you in any way."

"Come on," Angel said. "For the solidarity."

48

"Okay," the quiet one said in English. "All-ri."

"And thou?" Pachi said.

"No," I said. "But many thanks. I will come to hear Angel some other Sunday. Next Easter, perhaps. I need a little sleep."

"It is a folly," Pachi said. "You will only feel worse."

"No. But many thanks and good night."

"*Salud,*" they said. "*Hasta pronto.*"

I listened to them going down the street. Angel was singing Latin in a happy reckless voice.

Portrait of a Lady

THEY DROVE into Lappeenranta in the early afternoon.

"Well," the short fat one said, "here we are. We'll just stop here a minute and then take you to the hotel."

She did not answer. Her face felt hard and breakable and she could feel her mouth set and curving down and the lips stiff with cold. I won't even move, she thought. She had been holding herself still for over an hour. If you did not move the pain that had come with the cold stayed where it was and you could get used to it. If you moved there would be a new pain like a bruise that was suddenly pressed, sometimes like a suddenly opened cut. She did not think but held herself with her legs close together and her arms tight across her chest, sitting very still under the two gray army blankets.

There did not seem to be any streets. There was just open snow between the low gray frame houses. The sky was gray like the houses and in another half hour, at four o'clock, the sky would be black. The sky changed from black to gray and from gray to black and there was little difference in the feeling between day and night. She had not seen the sun since the day the war started. That was a fine bright morning but since then there was only this sliding between two darknesses. It was no warmer in the daytime either.

The tall fat one said, "This is the barracks."

"Is it?" she said. She turned her head slowly and saw through the frosted window a row of long gray wooden houses, smaller square gray houses, and near at hand resting on the snow, a fleet of sleds like children's sleds painted blue and yellow and green and red. They looked like the rowboats tied up on the lake at Central Park.

"What are they for?" she said.

"A man can pull one," he said. "They use them for anything. Food or ammunition. Sometimes a man will bring back another man who is wounded."

She looked at them again. On the short upturned runners small boxes had been nailed and the sides of these painted: the sleds were as gay as toys and it was not easy to imagine a soldier in the white snow camouflage overall, ski-ing through the forest, pulling another man who was folded up and helpless.

The short fat one came out of the nearest house and got in beside her.

"We'll get you warm now," he said.

When they stopped in front of the hotel, she said, "You'll have to unwind me and pull me out, Benno. I'm stuck here."

The short one took off the blankets and for a minute
she felt naked and the air covered her as if she were
being scraped with ice. Then he leaned in and took her
hand and helped her towards the door of the Ford sedan.
She tried to laugh but her mouth did not open properly
and the sound came out as a shaky cough. Then she was
on her feet and moving in long stiff-legged steps to the
hotel. It did not seem any warmer inside and she thought,
Oh, my God, can't they heat anything in this country?
they *want* it to be cold.

"Where's the ladies' room, Benno?"

He asked at the desk and showed her and told her that
they would wait in the dining room and order coffee.

The weak bulb in the ceiling did not make the room
light but she could see her face in the mirror. She leaned
closer, resting her hands on the wash basin, and studied
her face. Her skin was a thick frozen uneven red and her
eyes seemed to have sunk in. She was used to being beautiful and she liked it and needed it: and she hated looking
this way, like meat she thought, even if only that fool
of a Benno and that nice ox Carl were there to see her.

Carl pulled a long slender bottle from the inside pocket
of his sheepskin coat. They had seen that the dining room
was empty. Alcohol was forbidden to the army in the
military zone: but civilians did not drink in public places
either. It was a self-imposed politeness towards the soldiers. Carl took a big mouthful of the aquavit and passed
the bottle to Benno, keeping the colorless liquid in his

mouth. He kept it there, burning his palate comfortably, and then swallowed it in a gulp. He shook his head a little with the pleasure of feeling himself grow warm. Then he stood up and began to unwind a long tan knitted scarf from his neck. He took off his coat and finally his fur cap and stood by the table, very big, very rosy, with a round agreeable dull middle-aged face, and slapped his hands together and felt the aquavit warming him inside.

The two men disliked each other but they had been together only two days and the dislike was not yet ready to change into hate. Perhaps there would be no time for that, perhaps the dislike would only have time to change into open rudeness or planned silences. Benno, who was small, heavy, middle-aged too, but gray where the other was pink, and an imitation where the other man was simply himself, wanted to make the woman know that he was of her class, he was not a provincial like this common Swedish-Finn who was driving them. For the two days that they had travelled together Benno talked of nightclubs in New York and fashionable resorts in France and Switzerland and people whom the woman had never met at any of these places. Benno assumed she would recognize their names and place him by his friends. Carl said nothing except to ask for directions. He handled the Ford sedan skillfully on the roads that were bands of smooth oil-stained ice.

Benno took two swallows of the aquavit, corked the bottle and gave it back to Carl. He saw a waitress coming out of the door by the kitchen and called to her to bring coffee for four.

"Why four?" Carl asked.

"I met Lahti there in the Commandant's office," Benno said. He behaved as if it were usual to meet Lahti and as if he knew him well. "I asked him to come along and have some coffee. Mrs. Maynard would be interested to meet him, for her articles."

"So would I," Carl said reverently. Lahti was the hero of the war then, when the war was only a week old. He was either the best pilot in Finland or the most successful. The Finns made a practice of not creating heroes: they assumed that all men who risked their lives for their country were equally important and they did not give out names to the press and they did not do much awarding of medals. But Lahti had brought down four Russian planes in one day and the Propaganda Ministry in Helsinki could not restrain itself from speaking of this triumph.

"Where is her husband?" Carl asked suddenly.

"Mrs. Maynard's? In New York, I suppose."

"I don't understand it," Carl said.

Benno looked at him with amusement. "Why not?"

"I would not let my wife go alone to a war. I would not let her go anyhow."

"You are not modern."

"Maybe," Carl said. "Think what could happen to her.

Anything could happen to her. She is a small, pretty woman."

"She travelled all over the world alone, before she married. Haven't you read her books?"

They told Benno at the Propaganda Ministry in Helsinki that Mrs. Maynard had written two books and was a famous journalist. Benno at once remembered the two books he had not read and said that of course he had followed Mrs. Maynard's writing in the American press for years. He was to escort Mrs. Maynard on a trip to the front and serve as her interpreter. Mrs. Maynard was valuable to Finland because of her public in both the States and England. Besides that, her husband was chairman of the board of directors of one of the largest oil companies in America. Benno could readily see that a very rich man would be close to the government of his country: that was the way it worked everywhere. Moreover in Finland there was the problem of the petrol stocks. In time of war no Finn could forget that all petrol was imported.

No one had bothered to tell Carl anything. Carl was a civilian like hundreds of others who had offered his time and his automobile to the government, to be used in any way they decided. He is an unpaid sort of chauffeur, Benno thought, there is no reason to discuss Mrs. Maynard with him.

"She is rich?" Carl asked.

"Very rich."

"Then I do not see why the man has allowed her to come if they do not need the money. It is not safe for a woman."

"She was here before the war started," Benno explained. "She came at the time of the negotiations with Russia. She came to write about that. Who knew the war was going to begin so quickly? Now she will write about the war and then she will go. I will take care of her. I have my orders."

You, Carl thought. You will take care of yourself.

She stopped in the doorway and looked around the dining room. White covered tables were set in four rows down the long length of the room. In the windows between the clean looped white curtains there were thin ferns in pots. The walls were gray and the floor was covered with a dark patterned oilcloth. The room was not cold but it looked cold and you would have to be drunk to raise your voice in such a place or make good jolly talk with any one at those bare tables.

Carl stood up and waited for her to cross the room. He had travelled only in Finland and Sweden and the women he knew in both countries looked much alike. They were heavily built women with blonde or mouse-colored hair and good ruddy skin and when you thought about going to bed with them it was like thinking of something hearty and noisy, like eating well and getting drunk. If you thought about going to bed with this woman you were frightened. He had been wondering most of the day what she smelled like. When he wrapped her up this morning, in the blankets in the back seat, she smelled of flowers but flowers from a hot country. When the cold made her face red he felt safer with her. But now her skin was pale again and she looked like a soft spoiled cat. Only you did not care if she was spoiled, you would spoil her some more yourself if you got the chance.

Her face was wide at the forehead and eyes and her chin was not sharp but it was pointed, and with the large dark-flecked green eyes and the heavy blinking lashes, the small pointed nose, and the straight dark-red painted mouth, she looked to him like a cat that watched everything. There was nothing about her looks that Carl really liked. He did not like the small hands and the red nails that matched her lipstick; he did not like those light doubting eyes, he did not like her hair. It was dark brown hair, not black because there were reddish shades in it, and she wore it tight and neat to her head with a smooth roll that started just under her ears and dipped down around at the back of her neck. She was of medium height and Carl thought there would be nothing to her, nothing that would make you sure she was a woman and you would always be afraid she would squash in your hands. He did not know her clothes were smart and he found they only exaggerated that business of her not looking like a woman. She looked like a boy except too fancy for a boy. She wore a black ski-suit that was perfectly cut and very warm and black ski boots. Her white sweater came up high around her neck and she had on a beaver greatcoat, with the hood now thrown back. When she put the brown fur hood up, and you saw her sitting in her blankets in the back seat, she looked like an Eskimo. No, she looked like a cat, it was only the hood that was like the Eskimos.

Benno knew how expensive she was and he admired expensiveness.

"We were waiting for you," he said.

He says everything useless one can possibly say, she thought. "Thank you," she said.

Carl said, "Want some aquavit? To warm up?"

"Have you some in here?"

He handed her the bottle.

Lahti watched from the door. The line of the woman's throat was arched and smooth and she drank quickly as if to finish before any one caught her. When she gave the bottle back to Carl she smiled at him and said, "We're a pair of old drunks."

Carl laughed with pleasure. They were companions now, they had a joke together and she liked aquavit. Perhaps that Benno would not spoil the trip after all.

Can this be the one? Lahti thought. He had come because Benno insisted before the garrison Commandant, saying that this woman was a famous American writer and it was Lahti's duty to Finland to speak with her. He imagined she would be old and majestic the way a famous woman writer should be, with coarse straight gray hair and a strong nose. He had not wanted to come; he did not like to talk ever and he did not like to talk to women at all.

The fat little liar, Lahti thought, so that's what the propaganda people call a famous American writer. He had an hour before he need return to the field and with young pretty women you could look at them, you did not have to talk.

She's not so young, he told himself. No, she's not too young inside anyhow. He had seen that happen in women's eyes before but not so fast, or not so fast with this kind of woman: with professionals, yes, but they were trained not to waste time. He had seen the eyes shock open like that and tremble and seem to fix. There was the mouth too: it looked redder and softer.

She heard Benno's voice, the familiar sticky voice, saying, "This is Lieutenant Lahti, Mrs. Maynard."

Oh, is it, is it? You didn't tell me, she thought, you didn't get me ready.

The tall man clicked his heels and bowed over her hand. She could not see beyond the surface of his eyes. She let her hand rest in his. She·was not shaking hands with him, she was feeling his skin and through his hand the warmth and solidness of his body. When he raised his head, her hand lay still in his and she was looking at him in that way he knew but did not expect to find here. He smiled at her, very slightly and only with his eyes: it was a smile of recognition. She took her hand away quickly.

But she did not say how-do-you-do or won't you sit down or would you like some coffee? Benno waited for her to speak and not understanding her silence, but not believing a woman like Mrs. Maynard could be rude, he thought of the simplest explanation. Mrs. Maynard did not know who Lahti was; she had taken offense at having a stranger come to her table.

She sat very quietly and studied her long oval dark-red nails. She felt him warm and breathing beside her. But not warm, she thought, except that he would be warm and comfortable and certain of himself when I am gray and sick with cold. Only that sort of warmth; not warm-ready, not giving any of himself away.

"You have heard of Lieutenant Lahti," the sticky voice said. "Captain Ormesson made the announcement at the Press Conference in Helsinki. You remember, of course. It is the greatest single feat of the war: four Russian planes in one day."

She turned then, with a bright triumphant smile. Benno had succeeded in making this man ridiculous in just a few sentences, Benno the master of the shaming and the wrong.

She could look at him now. It was her turn to smile.

"They talk too much," Lahti said. There was hate in his voice.

Oh, the pride, she thought; and she had no advantage of him. *We* must not speak of planes. *We* must not speak of war. *We* must keep our dirty mouths off something we don't understand.

Carl did not know what was happening but he did not like it.

"Sit down," he said, in the large cheerful common voice. "Sit down everybody. Have some coffee before it gets cold. Cookies? Will you have a cookie, Mrs. Maynard? These are the old Finnish special cakes, for eating with coffee. You want some coffee, don't you, Lieutenant? It is a cold day."

Lahti sat in the chair beside her because it was empty, but he did not pull it close to the table. He held himself as a man who is obeying orders. He refused the coffee and Carl's cigarettes.

"Mrs. Maynard is writing articles for America and England," Benno said. You could spread his voice on bread, she thought. "It is very interesting for her to have some eyewitness anecdotes about the aviation. Could you tell us something of your squadron, Lieutenant?"

"The squadron is good. They work hard," Lahti said.

I wish I could see his eyes, she thought. He would be looking at Benno now with flat cold animal eyes, the eyes to match the voice.

"I have been told that the Russians fly badly," she said.

61

"They say their pilots are very inexperienced. What was it I heard? One of the prisoners had only twenty flying hours?"

"They are very brave," he said. "They fly as God wills." What have you come here for, you three civilians, asking questions like fools? He was the fool: he could have refused to talk with them. It made him feel dirty and ashamed to listen to them and dirty and ashamed to sit with them and look at their soft grasping faces, as they waited for stories of death. He knew he would remember this for a long time and hate them. The great snow-covered field that looked as bare from the ground as from the sky was only three hours away on the ice roads. Under a hump of snow beside three pine trees was a door covered with white cloth. Twelve men lived inside in a warm cave that smelled of the freshly cut pine their bunks were made from. There was a radio and a guitar and they waited for the telephone bell that warned them to go out to the single seater monoplane pursuits that were hidden under tents or camouflaged pine bough shelters. None of those men would be such a fool as to sit here.

The woman was the worst. The woman knew what she was doing.

He had heard them talking but he did not follow the words. Now she said suddenly:

"Benno, I thought you had to telephone to Viipuri?"

Benno looked at his watch. There was no hurry, it would be foolish to drive on tonight. Mrs. Maynard had been half dead with the cold; she could not stand more today.

"Hadn't you better put the call in now?" she asked.

"If you like," Benno said, ignoring the rudeness and the order so that Carl would not see him humiliated.

"I better see my car does not freeze," Carl said. She knows what she wants, Carl thought, whatever it is.

The dining room was very quiet. Lahti turned in his chair and faced her, since they were alone. He looked at her thoroughly and slowly with no expression in his eyes. He looked at her as if she were a new piece of machinery, a make of plane perhaps that he had never seen before. He was still looking at her when she started to talk. Her voice sounded very light and unsteady.

"I haven't seen that uniform." Why do I have to say just the idiotic thing he expects?

The uniform was plain dark blue; are his shoulders really like that, she thought, is it possible? Why can't I look at him the way he looks at me? I want to see how he is made too. Only where did you start if you felt so strange and hurried, so wanting. There isn't time, she thought. Time for what? He turned to reach across the table for the coffee pot. Look at the back of his head, she thought, just look at it. No, it's the way he moves, she decided, there is nothing wasted.

"It is the uniform of the aviation," he said. She had forgotten what they were talking about.

"Are you going to be here a few days?"

"I return tonight."

"Where?"

"To my squadron."

"Early?"

"Yes," he said. There had been eagerness and regret in her voice. What did she want, so fast? He would like to watch her if there were other men around; he would like to look at her and think about her but he did not want to talk to her by himself.

"We are going down to Karelia," she said.

"What for?"

"To visit the front."

"What will you do there?" he asked in amazement.

"Look at it, and ask questions."

"And then?" he said.

"Write about it."

"Oh." Did they do that sort of thing in the army, really? It seemed impossible. He could imagine what they would do at the field if a woman showed up when they had to fly and stood about looking at things and asking questions and getting in the way. They weren't really going to let her go down there in the woods, out in front of the Mannerheim Line?

"Do you do much of this work?"

"No," she said. "This is my first war."

As if it were the opera, he said to himself, or like going to the ski-jumping contests. Let those two civilians come back and nurse her.

64

"Tourism," he said.

"It makes good propaganda, you know, the writing, and that helps your country." Oh, like me, she thought. Like me now. Please. Look at me just once as if you could like me.

"Excuse me. We are glad for the help."

"Do you have to go back early tonight?" What am I saying, she thought. What am I doing? But if he goes, how will I ever find him again? I can't touch him at all; he doesn't need anything. But how would he be if he did need something? How would he be if he were like other men? Why won't he even *see* me?

"What is it?" he asked.

"I said, couldn't you stay over tonight?"

He smiled at her nicely. She is like a little stupid spoiled child, he thought. Perhaps she is making a collection of Finns to write about, or perhaps she thinks I will explain the aviation to her. She is funny and silly really, reaching out for anything she sees.

"No," he said.

"No," he said again. "There is the war, you see. We are engaged in that. The Russians come over sometimes six times a day. We have to be there."

"When are you going back?"

She is crazy, Lahti thought, but I have nothing to worry about any more.

"I am going now," he said.

He stood up and she looked at him but he was too high

65

above her. There is nothing I can do, she thought. He doesn't need anything.

She pushed her chair back and got up slowly.

She is just a spoiled beautiful crazy who travels around wanting anything she sees. So, he thought, let us oblige the famous foreign war correspondent. He reached out and put his hand on the back of her head, with his fingers tight over the dark hair. He pulled her towards him and held her head back and kissed her on the mouth. He did not kiss her in any particular way and then he waited a moment, smiling at her, and then he walked out of the room. She turned away from him. She felt sick-ashamed that he should have seen what she wanted and given it to her so casually.

They drove out of Viipuri the first night, following the shine and the feel of the car tracks. Even in that blackness you could tell that the houses on the street above the railroad station were gutted by bombs. The chains on the tires broke up the glass that had fallen into the street. The road curved up a hill and that was the end of the city. Then the road became a path of ice between solid black forest. It took two hours to go thirty kilometers to the first staff headquarters.

You could see the fires reflected in the little lakes. The lakes were like flat holes in the forest. The peasants set fire to their haystacks before they left. When the sky

66

was very pink, it would be a burning farmhouse. All the forest was silent and the road was empty. They moved slowly, afraid of the iced road.

When they stopped the car she did not see a path. They walked into a clearing and the round white tents were humps in the snow. The men were sleeping and they grumbled as they woke. They had been lying on straw, in a circle, with their feet toward the stove. There were twenty-four men in the tent. When they saw it was a woman they sat up straight and stared at her. They were boys, not men at all, young boys with tired eyes. This was out in front of the Mannerheim Line. They had been fighting a retreating action for five days, fighting like Indians, in small bands scattered through the forest. They slept again as she stooped to leave the tent.

The bridges were mined and the road was very narrow. The soldier who had joined them as guide at staff head-quarters spoke to Carl in a whisper. He was telling Carl to be careful at the bridges, not to skid. Carl whispered too. The forest went on forever and there was no noise. It was not like war, it was like being in the jungle at night, in a frozen jungle, knowing the animals could see you, feeling that the animals were waiting.

Then they heard the booming of the shells; the explosions were not far away but the sound was swallowed up in the forest and the snow. The booming spread over the sky in front of them like the light of the fires. Now the

67

whole sky was booming, slowly, with a deep spreading hollow roar. You did not know where the noise came from but it did not seem to come closer.

They were awake in this tent though it was past midnight. There was a field telephone and two men working over a map. The Colonel sat on a wooden box close to the stove and listened to what the telephone operator said and listened to the comments of the men studying the map. Two officers slept on the straw bunks at the side of the tent. One of the officers was writing a letter, with a three-legged low stool for a desk. It was warm and quiet inside the tent and calm.

An attack had just started, the first of any importance they had made. They were using two ski battalions; one battalion attacking the Russians from the rear, passing through the Russian lines to surprise them in the black frozen noiseless forest. It was warm here and she sat on the straw with her legs out towards the fire and smoked and waited while Benno talked.

"Ours," the Colonel said and there was a loud coughing barking roar near them, to the left in the forest. Their own artillery was answering the spreading boom of the Russians. Now it sounded like drums, almost regular in its beat, the near coughing sighing tearing outgoing shell answered by the never closer round loud dull roar of the incomer.

There were two cars, the one in front, a staff car, painted dead white for camouflage. Their black Ford sedan seemed to her garish and dangerous. They did not talk in the cars. At a bend in the road Carl halted, on whispered orders from their guide. Then suddenly he stepped on the accelerator and the car swung forward, the wheels grinding a little on the ice, then catching, and they speeded down an open stretch of road alongside a bare field. "They keep this piece of the road under shell fire," the guide said, "not very accurate."

The cars stopped, tilting sideways in the snow ditch. The soldiers were lined up on the other side of the road. She could not see the head of the line. They were motionless and silent and only their faces showed as a darkness against the snow, dark in the night. Then one man bent down to tighten the strap on his skis: another twisted to look behind him along the length of the line. They did not speak together. They were quiet with the held-in, absolutely still, waiting, tight concentration of before an attack. She did not go closer to them and there were no questions to ask and nothing to say. Then there was a slurring noise of skis moving on hard snow, a light irregular clink as if rifles hit against metal cartridge boxes, and one low word carried back from the front man from mouth to mouth, cold and soft: a word she did not understand.

"What is it?" she said, feeling her heart so loud and so heavy inside her that it was hard to breathe.

"Follow," the guide said, saying it exactly as the men did in the line.

"We must get out of here," Benno said. His voice was breathless with the choked windy sound of panic. "We are less than a kilometer from the Russians. As soon as the attack starts they will shell here, all this road. It is ridiculous for you to be here at all," the panic turning into anger.

She did not move. Benno was nothing here. Then a young officer took her arm and led her back to the Ford. She wanted to keep him with her, to hold tightly on to him; she was afraid but it was not fear that made her hold his arm, pressing it against her so that she could feel its hardness through her coat. I am here, she thought, I am here where no one has been. I know them, I have seen it and heard it and I am the only one. It could never be like this twice. The young officer looked down at her, trying to see her face. She did not seem to be afraid but she was trembling. This first big night attack was his business. He had no time to think of anything else. Why didn't she come tomorrow, when it would all be over?

The road was clogging up with ammunition sleds and Red Cross sleds. She had not seen any wounded. She did not know what this attack would look like when it started. She did not know that the soldiers would slip through the trees until they found the encamped Russians: that first it would be silent, the Finns in their white ski overalls sliding out from the night and then the wakened unready Russians and the Finns locked together and the wide-bladed Finnish knives: that first. War

70

seemed to her now a strange technical business, impossible to understand. It was like a fierce orderly quiet hunt: the skilled hunter tracking the deadly animal. She sat far back in the car and felt the cold really taking her now so that the pain of it went away and her life became smaller and smaller, frozen deep into her body. The cold was like dying.

Then it should have been dawn only they did not have dawn. Benno pounded on her door and came into the room.

"Get up at once. They will be over in ten minutes."

"I just went to bed," she said furiously. "I haven't slept two hours."

"I cannot take the responsibility of allowing you to stay here." He was trying to put it off on his job, on his orders. His face was gray. "We are on the sixth floor. The railway station is opposite. They bomb every morning at seven. It is always the same. They are aiming for the station."

The thin high screaming of the siren came through the windows that were closed with iron shutters. She had slept with the light on, dressed, just getting into the bed and going off into a sudden deep blackness of sleep.

"I will wait downstairs," Benno said. "Hurry, hurry; they will be here at once."

She could hear him running down the hall. He had left the door open. She heard the futile buzzing of the elevator bell and then she heard his boots clopping down the marble stairs.

He'll break his neck, she thought, a man so afraid ought not to run down stairs.

Now the hotel was very quiet, waiting for the planes. I wish I could see out the window, she thought, if only they knew how horrible it is to get bombed when you can't see anything. Shelters were the worst of all: you felt buried already, you waited for the roof to cave in, for the roar you would not even hear when it came.

She was cold and she was afraid. The siren went on rising and falling and she thought how no one, meaning to, could have invented a sound more like doom. Outside, Viipuri lay in the morning darkness, quiet and empty, with broken glass shining in the streets and bombed houses that looked like a black toothless opened mouth.

She combed her hair from pride, to keep herself slow, to keep from running. It was harder when you were alone. If there were other people around, anger helped you. You felt a sort of rage to be forced to behave badly in front of strangers. But even alone if you could control your fear you were all right. You could not stop it but you could hold it, you could make it do as you wished.

She walked down the stairs, thinking of Benno's loud fast-hammering boots. There was no one in the hotel lobby or on the street in front of the open door. A red arrow was painted on the side of the building: that would mean the air-raid shelter. The siren still stretched out, like wire through the air, but there had been no bomb explosions nor the humming closer and closer, wasplike first, then like a locomotive, throb of the plane motors. She could see nothing in the black thick sky. She walked towards the shelter and saw that it was the hotel garage and that twenty or thirty men, civilians, were waiting just inside the garage door with their faces turned up to the sky.

She had lit a cigarette and a man said to her, "Not smoke here," so she stayed outside the door, leaning against the wall and she forced herself to hold the cigarette easily and to smoke without haste. She watched herself smoking and hated the indignity of fear, the helplessness of waiting on a street for something you could not see, for so haphazard and impersonal a destruction.

When the explosions came they were not close, not very loud, and being so definite, so fixed, so distant, they seemed contemptible after the pain of the siren.

Benno hurried her, saying, "We must get out of town before the next raid, they come over all morning, hurry, get in the car, we'll have breakfast at the next village."

She was tired now and did not care; she was too tired and always too cold to want food and she hated Benno. She did not want him to take her arm or talk to her. It was easier to agree. He had no right to spread his fear like a disease, like a terrible killing disease: it was hard enough to handle your own fear and keep it down where it would not shame you. She rode in the front seat with Carl, saying that it was warmer and more comfortable. Benno, looking at her eyes, did not argue.

Then she slept against Carl's shoulder and did not see

the country which was like all the other country she had seen, the flat snow fields, the regular solid black forest and the odd-shaped flat lakes. She did not see the fog that came down towards nine o'clock and settled over the fields and the trees and the road so that you could not see more than ten feet ahead. It was a fog as thick as flannel and it meant the Russians would not fly.

"Here we are," Carl said. He shrugged his shoulder gently and she shook her head and waked. "We're stopping here for lunch."

Benno was already out and had gone in the front door. She saw the fog thicker than snow and coming out of the fog, with nothing around it, an inexplicable building, large, handsome, white, very modern, with large windows and a flat roof.

"What is it?"

"The officers club."

"What officers?"

"The aviation."

"Where are we?" she said.

"Benno does not allow you to have military information."

"Oh, Carl."

"Imatra," he said, "or near there. I don't know anything about it. I'm not a general like Benno. In peace, there used to be a military flying field near here and this is where the officers eat."

"Have we been on the road a long time?"

"Not long, just since morning. It is noon now."

"All right," she said, "I wish I could sleep. Benno seems to think sleep is just a quaint invention of mine."

"They have beds here."

"I hope they're good."

Inside it was new, clean, bare, steam-heated but cold, with the fog white against the long windows, with high empty walls and a polished rugless floor. There were modern deep square chairs placed in a semicircle around a coffee table at one end of the long room. The smorgasbord was laid out on a table in the center of the room and a serving table with silver chafing dishes stood along the near wall. There were four tables spread with linen and silver and in the great room the officers looked like fine military figures painted in a mural for a new airport. She gave her coat to an orderly at the door, and sleepy and cold and not used to this place she walked into the room and saw first of all Lahti, with his back to her, looking out the broad strip of the windows at the fog.

A man in a gray uniform with gray hair and a closely shaved pale face came forward, bowed over her hand and welcomed her in French. She thanked him but she was watching Lahti. She did not want Lahti to see her like this, mussed with sleep and still awkward from cold. Then he turned and saw her. He came across the room slowly and he was thinking that now she had come here to be a nuisance with the aviation as she had probably been with the army. But when he saw her face, he smiled at her for the first time, with liking and warmth.

"How was it in Karelia?" he said.

"You know Lieutenant Lahti?" the Colonel said.

"We met a few days ago."

"How was it in Karelia?" he said again.

"I don't know." How was it? It was cold and it was dark. It was stranger than anything she had ever seen or imagined. She did not know how you would have to feel to be able to fight like that. She did not understand the fighting itself. Men moved about in the darkness and fires burned on the small lakes. Today there would be some sort of change on a military map but she could not even read the map. She did not know where the Russians had been: there were no trenches, no fixed lines. Men hid in the forest and hunted each other.

Lahti thought she meant she did not know how the war was going and he liked her for not claiming to know. As a woman and a foreigner besides, she would have no right to speak of the war. He liked her face now too, without paint on it and marked with tiredness. He liked the way she had lost her certainty. He imagined the days in Karelia had taught her what this war was about and now she felt it with them, and was one of them, not a visitor who had come to take notes on disaster.

"You must drink something warm," the Colonel said. "Your friend Vuotso tells me you have been up all night

76

and that you left Viipuri after only two hours sleep."

"Yes."

"Then shall we sit down at .this table?"

Lahti sat opposite her. She was very tired but the hot coffee made her feel more alive and then less tired. She looked at Lahti, watching how he turned his head to listen to Benno, and examining the shape of his hands and seeing again the shape of his shoulders. Benno was bragging. She understood the bragging now. It was how he talked to talk down his cowardice. She was ashamed to be with him and she hoped the two men, Lahti and the Colonel, would know she had no responsibility for Benno nor for how he talked.

Then they were talking about the fog. We will have it all day, the Colonel was saying, it is a nice rest. There have been no alarms for four hours. It is useless for them to fly, they can see nothing. They cannot fly accurately by instruments, I think, at least they do not come over at night.

So Lahti would be staying here, probably. Would he? She stopped listening again and let herself go in the curious slow hidden excitement. She was not putting anything into words: she would make no admissions to herself. But now, watching him, she could feel it coming back.

Also, she thought suddenly, I have not sent a cable to Charles for five days. But then Charles knew she could always manage. Charles was charming, good-looking, and

fifteen years older than she. Charles did not go in for
worry. They agreed, four years ago when they married,
not to be like other people. They would not bore and
hamper each other the way most married people did; they
would go on with their two lives and be quite free. He
provided her with his valuable name and the solidness of
his money. In return, she was the great ornament of his
life. They had never discussed the terms of their bargain
and it worked very well. I'll cable Charles tomorrow, she
thought, he wouldn't like people to think he didn't hear
from me.

Suddenly she stood up and pushed her chair back from
the table. The Colonel looked at her in surprise and then
all three men rose.

"I want to rest." Why should I take this damned lack
of consideration from every man in Finland, she thought.
"I am very tired. Can you give me some place to rest?"

"But certainly," the Colonel said. "I am sorry not to
have spoken of it before. Lahti, will you take Mrs. Maynard upstairs? The large room at the end of the corridor
is ready. I will find the servant and have him build a fire.
We are short of servants now, Mrs. Maynard. They are
needed for other work. Will you excuse me for not accompanying you, while I make arrangements? You will
stay the night?"

"Thank you."

Lahti had already started across the room. What a
woman, he thought, she seems decent and suddenly she

behaves again like a spoiled mean lap-dog. He waited at the foot of the stairs and he thought: I would like to give her a good beating to teach her manners and to teach her that this war is not run for visiting women and if she comes, when no one asked her, she can at least behave.

He walked ahead of her down the corridor and she followed without speaking. He held open a door and she saw a room furnished in dark good conventional modern furniture. He did not come in.

"The servant will build the fire. I hope you are pleased with your quarters. They are, naturally, the best we have."

"Will you be staying here?"

"Overnight," he said. How she pried, how greedy she was, how she grabbed at you. He thought she was ugly when her face got this way.

"I will see you later."

"Yes."

He shut the door and walked down the hall fast, thinking that there was something very wrong with this woman, she could suddenly make you want to wash or to talk with men, she could make you feel as if there was a price on your services and she was used to buying anything she fancied. Couldn't she find men to satisfy her wherever she was before?

She stood in the center of the room, looking at it. They would send up her bag and build a fire. What if there were hot water? The bathroom was a pleasure to see and the water was actually hot. She would have all afternoon

to shed this cold disarranged bewildered self. It was good
to have a little time and be able to think. And there would
be no bombing while the fog lasted. She lay in the tub and
listened to the servant fix the fire and when he had gone
she could hear the wood crackling through the closed
bathroom door.

But why, she thought, why does he look at me like
that? He liked me and then he looked at me as if I were
ugly. It was not possible. He could not dislike her face or
her body. How could he? They were very good, they always had been, it was the thing she was surest of. He
ought to be grateful to me if nothing more, she thought
furiously, he ought at least to treat me with some kind of
respect. Nobody else would come to this unbearable country and really go out and see their war: there isn't any
one here who counts, I'm the only one who can be of
service to them. Who does he think I am? If he doesn't
know he might find out, he might stop being so conceited
and frozen and ask any one to tell him. Does he think
it's a whirl of gayety to be sick with cold and dead tired
and get bombed and shot-at and all the rest: doesn't he
realize what I can do for his war?

Not only the writing, she thought, though even he
ought to realize the value of it. I'm going to work for
them. I'll see Dickie and Tony in London and we'll plan
it out together. Of course they need planes: well, who else
can get in to the right people in London and Paris with a
first-hand account of what's happening? Even Washing-

ton, she thought, I'll spend months on it. He could be civil if only on that basis: what I can and will do to help them.

She turned on the hot-water tap with her toes but she was not resting as she had planned and she could feel, with irritation, how tight her forehead was and how her whole body was drawn up and nervous. I ought to sleep, she thought. I'll never get over this trip, my skin is practically ruined. I've already helped them: he could give me a little credit for that. I wrote about the negotiations. I put the blame squarely on the Russians: I made it very clear so there was no chance of any one imagining the Finns had been obstinate or provoking. If he knew how twisted things can get and how hard it is to change public opinion once it starts off wrong, then he'd thank me. And that article about the first day's bombing in Helsinki, well, my God, they couldn't buy such propaganda. Charles cabled me that the Red Cross was making a drive to help Finland; he said my piece was a sensation in New York, every one was furious, every one in Washington even was stirred up. And who else was here to write? Another open city bombed and more civilians killed. The readers are used to that now. They don't want to hear about it unless it's given to them in some way they can't ignore. You have to have a name to be noticed, she thought, raging against Lahti: why is he so damned stupid?

And now I'll do at least three pieces about this trip to Karelia and everybody will know how wonderful the army is and the aviation too naturally, and that help must be sent because the Finns *can* hold out (and what in God's name is more useful for them than that?) and besides I'll tell the necessary people myself and insist on it. Well, then, what right has he to be so bloody patronizing?

Oh, damn it to hell, she said to herself, stop thinking about him. I can't, she thought, I can't, I can't. She lay back in the hot water and tried to empty her mind and tried to relax the muscles of her face so that they would not hold these tight lines of anger and disappointment. Then quite suddenly a story took shape in her mind; it was easy as dreams are.

She would stay here and Lahti would love her because he would believe in her; he would see that she was as good as he was and no more afraid than he and she would do something that he could understand and admire. Evidently he did not understand what she was doing now. She would volunteer for one of those services the women of the Lotta Svard did: she would stand for six hours at a time on the roofs, wearing the white camouflage overall, to watch for planes and sound the air-raid signals. And when she came back at night he would see how tired she was and know what she had been doing and he would love her and she would stay here and the nights he was not flying, or she was not on duty, they would spend together. They would have it like that, the war belonging to them both, and he would love her the way he must, in his own way, not talking, but with those flat strange terrifying eyes owning her and wanting her.

The women she knew would say Ann's mad, she's gone out of her head; but they would be wild with envy, not knowing what he looked like or how he was but guessing how he must be to keep her here. And they would know too that nothing like this would ever happen to them, nothing final and dangerous and so strong that you did not need all the trivial things they needed. Poor Charles, she thought, but then she was thinking about the scandal and how it would upset him. Only it wouldn't be a scandal, it would be a love story. She was not taking anything away from Charles because they had never been like that: they never could be. She did not have to feel guilty. Charles doesn't really love me, she thought, or he'd be on his way here now. He loves me as much as he knows how but it is nothing like this. Why can't Lahti *see,* why won't he even look at me?

I ought to file my first story about Karelia at once, she thought. It will be in ahead of every one. I'll have to go to Helsinki to do it because of the censorship. I can come right back afterwards but that certainly has to be done tomorrow. How can I write when I'm so tired? He might help me a little; he isn't the only one who is working for Finland. How can he be so hard and so unkind when after all I've been doing everything I can for them and I'm going to stick with it and it certainly isn't something for myself, it's because I feel I must help them, I want to. If nothing else, he might realize I'm alone here and it isn't easy to be alone with bombs falling and shells exploding

and he can't expect me to be used to all that; where would
I have gotten any experience of it before? Does he expect
me to be made of iron and never get tired and never get
frightened and I'm not a Finn, it isn't as if I had to be
here.

She stood up and found the air very cold after the hot
water and she dried herself, rubbing the towel hard over
her body. No bath salts, she thought, no oil, no cologne,
no nothing. Oh, I'm too tired. Damn him anyhow, what
kind of a man is he?

She put on pyjamas and a dressing gown and went into
the bedroom. The sky was already smearing from gray to
black. I hate this place, she thought, how can people live
when it's night all the time? The fire was burning down
and the walls were shadowed with firelight. The bed
looked soft but she knew that she would lie stiff and aching between the sheets until she could warm them with
her body and even then she was never really warm. I'm
tired and I'm lonely and Benno's a coward and Carl is a
bore and I have to write a good piece tomorrow and I'll
be dead tired and he acts as if I were here for fun. I'd like
to see any other woman going through this. She kicked
off her fur bedroom slippers and climbed into the bed.
The sheets made her teeth click together with cold and
she lay down, rigid under the covers, holding herself tight
together with her knees against her stomach and her feet
wrapped in the ends of the woollen dressing gown.

I don't even know his first name, she thought, and he

wouldn't give me a chance to tell him what I plan to do for Finland. If I start crying just because everything's so bleak, I'll really be ugly. Not that he would care, not that he cares if I can ever sleep or not, not that he cares. She turned her face away from the darkening windows and the sliding shadows of the fire and pulled the covers high around her throat.

The telephone bell woke her. The fire had died down and the room was black and she did not know where she was. Then she thought the telephone bell was an air-raid warning and she listened for the planes and she was frightened because she did not know how to get out of this place. The telephone rang again. She groped for the bedside table and found the telephone and heard Benno's syrupy voice, telling her that the gentlemen were waiting, would she come down to dinner.

"In half an hour," she said. And they won't have a thing to drink and most of them will not talk any known language, though dear old Benno will of course talk without stopping in that voice that makes you want to scream. But Lahti will be there, she thought. Where is the light? I haven't anything to wear. My clothes will take root and grow on me pretty soon.

She found the light and went into the bathroom where the good mirrors were and she saw that her face looked fresh and rested, though the eyes were a little swollen with sleep.

Would it be better to leave off the mascara and go down

85

with my eyes looking shiny and crinkled up? I could brush out my hair, she thought, and wear it as I used to, sort of aimless and fluffy. But then she thought, no, no, it won't do, that isn't my genre any more. There's nothing in that suitcase. I should not have listened to Benno and his pompous orders. There was plenty of room in the car for another bag.

She emptied her suitcase on to the bed. How can I combine it? she thought. The silk shirt was the only soft-looking thing. How about the heavy white silk shirt, worn opened and opened low, and her hair put up as if for evening clothes, and her eyelashes very black and heavy and a very red mouth but no other make-up, and the small pear-shaped diamond earrings? She had brought few jewels to Finland and then decided they would be safer travelling with her: the Helsinki hotel might be bombed while she was in Karelia. Those little drops of diamonds, that just made a radiance at the tips of her ears, would change the whole get-up into something amusing. She would be chic and at the same time feminine to the waist, and the black ski-pants and boots would be a reminder of where she had been these last days. You could not be too elegant: they resented it. They seemed to think you were forgetting their war if you simply tried to make an evening less dreary by dressing properly.

Now, standing in front of the long mirror she considered and approved her reflection. I look ready for the Duchin room at Sun Valley, she thought, after a day's ski-

86

ing; or for cocktails in the bar at Saint Moritz. This is very good. This will do perfectly. At Saint Moritz, Lucy Barnham always wore enormous diamond clips on a silk shirt when she came in from ski-ing or from pretending to ski. The clips were too big really, too flashing and besides they weighed down the silk. The little earrings are just right. I must remember, she thought. It will be cold with nothing on except the shirt but the coat is too crumpled and I've even slept in it. A sweater would spoil the whole effect. Possibly they will light the fire downstairs as a concession to the frail foreigner. When you stopped to think about it, it was incredible how they behaved. Even being cold was a kind of insult to their country or an admission of inferiority.

They were waiting for her and as they did not drink, obeying the rules that mechanics and mess servants had to obey, they were waiting silently. She found Lahti at once and when she saw his eyes, she smiled. Carl noticed the smile and told himself again how like a cat she was. Lahti's eyes had widened and lighted. He had not thought of her at all but only responded with pleasure to the small pointed face and his eyes proved too that he had not missed the uptilted sharp curve of her breasts, beneath the white silk, nor the straight line of her hips. Then he looked at her face again and saw her smile and realized she had been waiting confidently for his admiration and his eyes went flat and hard. But she had seen the first shock of his pleasure and she did not care.

The Colonel asked how she had rested. She was very charming because she remembered that she had spoken crossly after lunch. Three young officers, from Lahti's squadron, watched her with open admiring faces. They were introduced but they spoke no language she spoke. She noted how young they were and she thought briefly that it was remarkable that such children could fly and then she turned to talk again with the Colonel.

For the last hour, Lahti had been discussing with Colonel Sala how to bring over four pursuit planes which were waiting at Oslo. Four was very few, considering that in all Finland they had only a hundred planes, but perhaps these four were the beginning, they had to be the beginning. The English would send more: the French too, surely. If they crated the planes there would be the slow rail passage across Norway and Sweden and the danger of some complication at the frontiers. If they flew them there would be two refuellings in Sweden, the condition of the Swedish fields to consider, and the weather. The weather was generally bad now, it was the season of fogs.

But could they spare four men to go and get the planes? Pilots were scarce too. It had to be thought out from every angle and decided at once. The Colonel wanted Lahti to go himself and take these three young pilots with him. Even four planes were so valuable that it was worthwhile to turn over the squadron to Koivo for a few days. Koivo is a good man, Colonel Sala said. Lahti was not worried about that. Any man in his squadron was as good as he was, for that matter. Only he belonged here. He did not want to be in Oslo when the morning patrol went out over Karelia.

Still they had to have replacements. They had lost two planes already. Why not send Koivo? You have more experience, the Colonel said. Four planes. We could not afford to lose them for any reason. If only the Swedes or the Norwegians would take on the job, Lahti thought, instead of sitting at home and shouting about their sympathy and their neutrality.

In any case, they had to get back to the field at three this morning and be ready for the early patrol over Viipuri and Karelia. After the first patrol he could arrange how the work should be divided so as to make the loss of four pilots less serious. Perhaps some relief pilots could fly down from the central sector though that was doubtful because the Russian attack was heavy there. Mannerheim himself had his headquarters somewhere east of Oulu. There were no unneeded pilots anywhere. Above all the thing to do is not waste time. Sala wants the planes flown in, he thought, it is up to me to get them and the quickest way is to do it myself. He and the three who were here tonight, competent boys but with less experience than some others in the squadron, would leave for Turku after dark tomorrow and with any luck at all they should be in Oslo the day after. No one would think he was taking a soft job, to get out of it for a few days. Three days probably, he told himself, Koivo will manage without us.

The Russians have not sent over more than two squadrons at a time, thus far. It is better to go now.

These plans stayed in his mind and he watched the woman and thought that if he had time he could hate her for the way she entered a room, demanding every one's attention, forcing herself and her body on them all, who had no right to weaken themselves with desire, who had given that up because there was no place for it now. The three boys from his squadron were his friends: he knew what they had to do every day. And now she came, almost naked, he thought furiously, to disturb them, to make them want what they could not have, to make their work harder. He saw how they were looking at her and he hated her and the criminal idiots in Helsinki who would send a high-class whore when no one could profit from her but all could be made uneasy and restless and confused by her presence.

She sat at the head of the table with the Colonel at her right and Lahti at her left and Benno and Carl farther down. The Colonel included Lahti because he was glad of assistance and a man who could speak English. The officers sitting at the other small tables spoke together rarely and softly in Finnish. They were listening for the woman's voice though they could not understand what she said. They waited for that low almost singing sound of the woman talking. The officers who could look at her without turning or without attracting her attention watched her steadily. One of the three young pilots, sitting at the table nearest her, thought he could smell her perfume: it was the same perfume that seemed so rare and lovely to Carl, made from the flowers of a hot country.

The Colonel, at any rate, understood what her work was and the importance of it. She had asked him about their planes and the Russian planes and to her surprise (because though she resented it, she was becoming accustomed to the Finnish manner towards journalists), he answered her well. Now she was listening, with care, remembering it all for her articles. Lahti marvelled at this change: look at her, he thought, she actually cares about this, she is not making conversation. What for; and can she understand what she hears?

She knew nothing about aviation but she would remember, as she had always remembered, what she needed to know. Later, writing it accurately and with great assurance, it would seem that she herself was an authority on these planes. The Colonel was speaking of the Russian bombers. She fixed her memory on the words. The Russian bombers were the S.B. and D.B. model. The S.B. had a top·speed of 280 kilometers an hour, the D.B. made 350 kilometers an hour. They were too slow, patterned after a Martin bomber that was no longer used in the States, and they could not fly above 8000 meters whereas the Finnish pursuit which were single seater monoplanes made in Holland surpassed the Russian bombers both in speed and altitude.

It was difficult for her to ask questions because there was Lahti waiting, she thought, waiting for me to be ignorant. Why shouldn't I be ignorant? What does he know of the things I know? She went cautiously, trying to ask questions which would at least seem reasonable.

"What weight bombs do the Russians use?" she said.

"The bombs have not been very heavy here. In Helsinki itself, it is a different matter. Around here, and principally over this front, they are using 50-kilo bombs. Their bombers carry 1000-kilo loads."

She liked the Colonel. He answered questions clearly and as he answered them, she saw that the questions were good. Benno listened respectfully and Carl listened with interest and Lahti watched them all, wondering at the courtesy and patience of Colonel Sala and wondering at the woman's insistence. She is very rare, he thought, and how different her eyes are now: quick and sharp and thinking but impersonal. She wants nothing of Sala except facts.

"Where do the Russians come from? I mean where is their field?"

"We think they come from Novgorod."

Look up Novgorod on the map, she noted.

"It is too far off to permit them to have accompanying pursuit."

"You mean the bombers fly alone, without any fighter planes?" she said.

"Yes."

"I saw some anti-aircraft guns the other day," she said. She did not know where she had seen them. That was· Benno's work. Benno was not exactly the perfect guide for a journalist. He would never tell her the names of places. "Military secrets," he would say, wearing an expression of loathsome mystery. Now she was angrily embarrassed that she could not say where she had seen these guns. "Are they effective against the bombers?" she asked. Without turning her head, she watched Lahti. She did not know whether this was a sensible question.

"We have pretty good luck," the Colonel said. "Those are Bofors guns, perhaps the best in the world, and our men know how to use them. The fog has forced the Russians to fly low all week. Yes, I think you could say we do well with the anti-aircraft."

They were interested and puzzled by the Russian flying.

"They must have a good aviation. We can only think they have not yet sent either their best pilots or their best planes."

"Oh," she said, not risking a question now. If only he would talk, she thought, without prompting. Maybe he will if I say nothing.

"Now here," the Colonel went on, "they have bombed the field regularly. Of course everything is underground and dispersed and camouflaged so there is no visible good target. There are the hangars from peace time but naturally we do not use them. They demolished the hangars but it took them many trips and the thermite bombs did the work. The hangars are burned, not truly destroyed with high explosive. They tear up the ground but miss the buildings. It is strange."

The Colonel waited. He had answered her questions neatly and politely but he was not giving her anything she did not ask for.

"I'd like to see the field," she said.

"You can go over tomorrow. Mr. Vuotso and Mr. Petersen will take you over. Lieutenant Lahti will leave permission with the field commandant."

Lahti said nothing. It was not his place to question decisions and surely not in front of civilians, but if he could see the Colonel alone he would explain to him that the woman should not come. She had done damage already. From where he sat he could see the face of Heikki, dazed and dreaming, forgetful of them all: Heikki who was not thinking but holding himself quietly so as not to lose any of the scent of her perfume.

She was eager for the meal to end now. She had learned all she needed to know and she wanted to write it down before she confused the figures. The room was cold too and there was nothing more to do here.

"Will you excuse me," she said. "We will be up early tomorrow to go to the field and then I must get back to Helsinki to send off an article. It is such a luxury to sleep these days, isn't it? You have been very kind to me. Shall I see you in the morning?"

"I will be here all day," the Colonel said.

"Then I'll wait to thank you until tomorrow. I appreciate all the help you've given me, Colonel Sala. Good night."

They stood up at their places and the Colonel said, "Lahti, you and your three should go to bed early too, as you must be off at two-thirty. I excuse you now."

"May I speak to you a moment, sir?"

"Very well, then. But we must not take much time."

The Colonel turned and spoke in Finnish to the three boys at the next table.

"They will escort you upstairs, Mrs. Maynard."

She smiled at the other officers, who rose and bowed, with the quick formal stiff-waisted bow that always amused and pleased her. The boys followed her. I am like a kindergarten teacher taking the children across the street, she thought. In the upstairs corridor they stood at a suitable distance from her door and bowed and smiled and finally one of them, blushing, said, "bon soir," and then they turned and hurried after each other into rooms farther down the hall.

She had thought about this without letting herself worry or make any precise plans. Now she undressed quickly and left her ski-boots near the door. She sat at the desk and made notes of what the Colonel had said and then she thought: I can ask him to verify these figures. I can say I am working on the article now and I did not want to disturb Colonel Sala. I can do that. Or I can say nothing. Wait, she told herself. Wait and see. Then she heard him walking down the hall. She went to the door and stood close to it and listened. She had picked up her boots and her heart was beating with excitement and a sort of fear. What if any one should see me, but no one could see me: what am I doing, she thought, if any one ever knew I'd done such a thing. She felt her face flushing and as the steps came closer she put her cool hand on her cheek and tried to breathe easily. I must be mad, she thought, I've never done such a thing in my life. It's too outrageous; I ought to be able to open the door and say, Good evening, I'll be coming in to see you later to get some help on this plane stuff. Now the steps had stopped.

She opened her door quietly and stooped and placed her ski-boots outside her door. If he saw her, that was what she was doing: surely a reasonable and honorable thing to do. As she rose she saw his back and saw the door closing behind him. He was staying in a room across the hall, three doors farther on. My fur slippers won't make any noise in the corridor. She shut her own door, holding the knob so that the lock would not click into place. Then she stood before the mirror in the bathroom, staring at her face but not seeing it, and she thought: what will happen? But I have to.

Lahti fixed his pillows and the lamp by the bed and started to read, knowing he could not sleep this early. The newspaper was two days old and had been sent down from Helsinki. He was reading about the attack in central Finland. The press announced Russian defeats. That was of course necessary. It was very bad there in the center and the Russians, though not advancing rapidly, were surely advancing. It did not matter how many of them died; there were always more Russians. They were trying to drive a wedge through to the Bothnian Gulf to cut the only railroad from Sweden, the one that came down along the coast from Tornio. He read of how the Russian tanks were held up and entire Russian battalions were encircled and annihilated and he thought how few kilometers separated the Russians from the railroad.

He tried to make himself read without that tight hurting worry. It is not my job, he thought, I have my own small work. I am not supposed to know everything and see everything. I am not supposed to .make myself such an important man that I can worry for all Finland. I have the responsibility for one squadron of pursuit planes and that is all I am ordered to do and that is all I am able to do. I am supposed to sleep so that I will fly well. They have better men to do the worrying.

It was all right to say it and in his head he understood and believed what he was saying and he knew that his squadron was enough for him and if every man did his own work that was the best way to save the country. He loved to fly. He knew what flying meant to the others, too. He knew all the things you felt, alone in the small plane. He knew that terrible shouting insane lonely wordless shaking blind joy of being alone against them, and

97

still flying, but they not flying, not any more, not now, and you were alone in that piece of the sky. It had nothing to do with the Russians really: they had spoken to the four Russian aviators who came down safely and were brought here for questioning. He had no feeling about the Russian pilots; as men, they did not count.

If he was at the field and with the others, he did not think. Here, waiting to sleep, he could think of this war and know how well it was going now and still know how few Finns there were. Always how few there were. He did not think about winning or losing the war. He thought, with pain, so that there was no room in him for thinking of anything else: we are very few.

His hands lay flat on the covers of the bed and the light shone down on his face and on the newspaper beside him and his face looked as it did every morning after the first patrol, when he was waiting to hear who had come back and who had not come back.

She opened the door softly and for a moment he could not see her by the door.

"I'm afraid," she said. "I'm lonely and I'm afraid."

Her voice was very young. He reached for the lamp, to turn it so that he could see her. She looked smaller and for a moment he gave in to the voice and to the words and he was ready to be kind with her. He was ready to believe her. Then he saw how lovely she had made herself and he thought of her again as some one who planned and reached out for what she wanted. She wore a wine red woollen dressing gown and the silk pyjamas were of the same color, but what he saw was the low opening at her throat and the dark straight line of shadow between her breasts.

"There is nothing to be afraid of here, at night," he said. "They do not come over at night."

"I'm cold."

He waited, smiling at her. She did not move. Oh, you, he thought, oh you soldiers' delight.

"What have I done to you?" she said. She means that anyhow, he thought.

"Come on," he said. "Why not?"

She went slowly towards the bed. She was looking at his face to see something that was not there.

"Take off your slippers and your coat."

He moved the pillows and held open the covers for her.

"Turn off the light," she said.

"Why?" And since when do they give orders, since when have they got anything to say about how it shall be done?

"Please."

"When I want to," he said.

"You hate me," she said with wonder.

"Not even that. Why are you selfish? There are three other pilots here. Don't you want to serve Finland?"

She knew she would not leave no matter what he said; he could talk to her this way all the time and she still would not leave but she felt sick inside herself that this was happening to her. She had not imagined it could be this way.

"All right. I'll turn off the light. What is the difference? It can do no harm. Only the loss of sleep. I have flown pretty well without sleep before."

Then she said, "But if you kiss me like that, it must mean something."

"Where did you learn to say such things?"

"I love you."

"If you talk, I will take you back to your room. It is all right but not with talking."

He turned off the light then, but he did it for himself. In the dark he could think anything he wanted. Her feet were cold and so were her hands and her body felt thin to him and hard and shut-in with cold. Then her skin felt cool and softer. Then her whole body was warm, not thin any more, but small, easy, easy to hold and warmer, warmer.

"Oh," she said, "oh, Lahti, Lahti. Tell me some name to say. Your name. I want to know your own name."

"You could not pronounce it," he said. Then angrily, wakened from the dream of warmth and softness, she with a voice becoming this woman, this particular woman and not all women, "Do not talk, I tell you."

Moving like water, he thought, and with that wonderful old, remembered always, new strangeness and softness so that you felt you were floating and anything could be true and you did not think but felt softly and all through you, without effort, every moment of it, slowly, slowly, the warmth and the softness and the woman smell, and the resting heavily but without weight. You had no body, it was as if together without bodies, but so closely that she pulled up with your breathing and she was not against you but in you and her hair against your mouth and now her lips.

Then it changed, as he knew, and what had been before was forgotten and there was only this fierceness like the down-diving plunge of the plane and a wildness and crying and force like the wind that beat up against you, and again, and she was gone, was nothing, and he was alone with the need and the unwaiting hurting deadly haste and the sinking down that would not end, that hurt him and drove him for an end. She was not there at all, and he was alone: ending, ending, with the two wheels of the plane just touching, scraping, bumping, rolling and now the plane was steady and grounded.

The room was still and airless. He turned away from her. Later she leaned over and touched him but he drew away from her hand. He did not know her. It was anybody's hand: it was unwelcome. She waited in the darkness, frightened but feeling strange and new and as if she had been waiting for a long time ignorantly and now she waited with knowledge.

She did not touch his body but she understood it, with this new knowledge. She thought once, triumphantly:

I know now. She could hear him breathing; he was not asleep but he was far away from her, waiting too. Then she touched him softly as if in question, and held herself tight with doubt and with wanting, and he moved towards her and his hands hurt her and she had no time to breathe and she was afraid and exultant and then she was nothing, caught up by him, part of him, all lost, carried, gone from herself, with nothing of her own left.

Then she was alone too, only breathing, making herself breathe, slowly, slowly, quietly, and her body was light and sea-weed soft and she thought: I will never leave him. He is mine now. Now he is mine.

"Are you asleep?"

"No," she said.

"Then you better go back to your room."

His voice shocked her the way the fear of the bombers did, into a blurred, panicked awakeness.

"No," she said, "no."

"I have work to do tomorrow." His voice was patient. His voice was casual. It can't be, she thought. Not now.

"I ought to sleep, or at least rest. I have an hour and a half before I must leave."

And there was only the tiredness, the sick empty tiredness. Who asked her? he thought. It isn't as if I was crazy for need of it; I wasn't. I was all right. I didn't need it. His arms felt heavy and dead; and there was the bitterness and the weakness of afterwards.

"When will I see you again? Tomorrow?"

"No," he said, "I am going away for a few days."

"Where?"

"Nowhere."

"Tell me."

"I am going on a shopping trip."

"But for how long?" she said. Oh no, oh no, not now. You can't go now.

"For three days, I think."

"In Helsinki?"

"No."

"But I will see you when you come back?"

Probably, he thought. Since those Propaganda fools in Helsinki do not seem to realize there is a war here.

"I will see you?" she said again.

"Oh, I don't know."

She held herself quiet, she would not let herself in for that voice and that way of speaking. She would be careful and it would not happen. He did not want to talk; that was it. She would be careful.

But three days: how can I? And then she thought: no, it is good. It is perfect. It turns out beautifully. I will go to Helsinki and cable my articles. Charles and every one will know then why I must stay. They will see it in what I write. They will understand that I belong here. I will cable Charles and tell him simply that I cannot leave, that it would be shameful to leave now. I must stay and do what I can. Then I can come back here; surely there are houses somewhere around, and I will take one and stay here. I can get used to the cold. It is only because I am not used to it that it seems so dreadful to me. I will stay here and work and I can get down to Karelia easily when I have to and I will do articles from time to time, when something big happens. After all, the writing is more useful to Finland than any little job I could do here in the country. And that way Charles and the others will see why I have to stay: and the Propaganda people will understand too. It is nearer the front and the real story here and I will see him at night. He never flies at night. And if I have my own house.

She moved close to him and kissed him where his throat made a hollow into his shoulder. "Lahti, I love you, I never loved any one before."

"You? You do not know what love is about."

It does not matter, she thought. He can speak that way now. He is afraid of me, he is afraid to love me. But in a week, in two weeks, in three weeks, he will not speak like that. He will know then.

"I do," she said, softly. "You will see."

"I will see nothing," he said. "This is the first and last time."

Oh, no, she thought, he is too proud, he is too cruel. He thinks too much of himself now. Later, I will remind him of this and make him sorry for it. Later he will beg me to forgive him for having spoken like this. Later when he wants me and is not so certain of getting what he wants.

"You will see what it is like to love," she said. I will

make you love me and you will love me so that you are never free of it and you will be afraid for having talked to me this way.

"I love many things," he said. She listened carefully. She had never heard this voice. But it had to happen, afterwards there had to be the telling and the giving: now the cruelty had gone from him and he was going to show himself to her.

"What do you love?" she said, being gentle with him.

"Nothing you would know about." She would even like to reach in and feel around my mind. She will take anything and everything.

"Please."

"I love a plane," he said. "I love any plane I fly."

Like loving my typewriter, she thought, with amusement: how very young he is.

But as she did not speak and as he was talking to himself, in his loneliness, he went on, "I love flying."

He saw it all now, what he loved, and speaking of it he got himself back and some of the weakness and sickness drained out of him.

"I love the men in my squadron."

That was a thing men always had, braggingly, absurdly, comically, this huge blown-up business of their friendship with other men. As if women could not love each other. She had never known a man who did not trot that out, sooner or later. It was a trick of their own, they must have learned it at school. They evidently felt it was necessary to say. All right darling, she thought, love them. Love them hard. In two weeks, in three weeks, you are going to love me: you won't be thinking of them then. I will buy things to make the house charming: the shops are still very good, surprisingly good, in Helsinki. He will come in at dark and stay most of the night and that is what he will love.

"And I love something else." She could scarcely hear him and for a moment she hated him, in jealousy. Some one else, she thought, one of those hearty Finnish girls with hips as wide as a chair and that awful scrubbed skin. One of those, no doubt. How could he be so tasteless and tiresome and middle-class; and he had slept with her probably, making sentimental conversation in Finnish while he did it. You couldn't be jealous of that, you could only be ashamed for him.

"What did she look like?" she said.

"What?"

"The one you loved."

"What one?"

"The Finnish girl."

"There have been some," he said. "All good. All honest. All women. I did not say I loved them. But afterwards, I could always look at them."

"Oh?" Oh, really, darling? What a child I have on my hands, she thought. She felt fine now, fine and confident. There was nothing to worry about. It would happen easily and wonderfully and without trouble. Cabling articles, from time to time, would be protection every way. She did not have to compete with those noble Finnish girls of his memory.

"So that is what you love, my dearest," she said. He was sweet really. "Your plane, flying, your squadron, and some fine Finnish girls."

"I did not speak of girls." Now she was taking it away and he needed it. He needed to know clearly what he had, he needed to make himself solid again before he went out to his work. And she was twisting that and making it cheap and harmful. I am tired, he thought, and I have no right to be.

"Not girls?"

"Be quiet," he said fiercely. "Do not speak of things you cannot understand."

"But tell me." Then it was something else and something she had not understood. She must know now, because knowing she could guard against it. Nothing must happen now. He spoke to her with a strange voice: casual, impatient, hating, bored. But she was not afraid of that. She could change that. It was only if there was something she did not know and it would come up suddenly later, when she was not prepared for it. She had to know everything tonight. Later she would fix it all: there would be no problems. Only she had to know.

She was not talking and in the dark room he was alone again, tired and knowing how dangerous the tiredness was and how wrong, as if he had cheated what he loved.

What he loved he could not truly cheat, though he could serve less well. But he had flown without sleep before. He knew always how to do it, not only with his mind, and he would do it well as on all the other days. He was very tired and he felt uncertainly that she had gone, and leaving the room she had gone away truly, beyond memory, beyond his anger or shame or regret. It was as if she had never happened. He was almost asleep now. The first patrol; and the second; and then the trip to the supply office because they needed a new stove in the dugout and then the talk with Sala. Twenty-four hours without sleep and soon it would start again but now he could sleep for a while, for long enough.

"What is it you love?" her voice came as a whisper, a voice in a dream.

"I love Finland," he said, murmured, with his eyes closed, almost asleep. "I love Finland."

"Of course," she said, pleasantly. So that was what it was: that was all right. "I love America, too." She spoke briskly and she wakened him and he remembered what he had said, what he would never say, and he hated her for dragging that out of him too. She took that too and that was his own. Then he remembered her voice and remembered with relief what she had answered and how she had not understood. She did not know what she had taken from him. It was of no value to her. So, in a way, it was as if he had said nothing.

Suddenly, so that he felt himself cold and dangerous

with it, he wanted to put his hands on her and close them and tighten them and hurt her slowly and terribly until really she would not be there, the high-class whore who made you do what you did not need to do and left you worn-out and useless and then took your secrets and threw them around as if they were without value.

"Get out," he said. She thought he was speaking into his pillow, his voice sounded so choked and low.

"You cannot sleep if I am here?"

"No."

"Poor darling."

She felt around for her slippers and found her dressing gown and stood up, dressing herself in the darkness.

"I'll see you in three days," she said. "Take care of yourself, beloved."

She was standing by the bed. He did not move and he did not want to see her, even as a shadow in the dark room. She had won, really. She would never be tired, she would never lose that confidence, she would never be hurt by anything because she would never recognize the things that could hurt.

"Shut the door," he said wearily. "Just shut the door."

She bumped into a chair crossing the room and laughed and he said, "For God's sake be quiet. You don't need to wake up the other three. You don't need to torment them with what they missed tonight."

I don't care, she thought, he can say whatever he pleases. Now. It does not touch me. This is only the beginning. Later he will be sorry for having been nasty; he will be terribly sorry.

She turned at the door to whisper good night to him. But he was unmoving and silent in the bed. He is asleep, she thought, poor boy, he only has an hour really. She was careful not to make any noise, crossing the hall to her own room.

The sun came in through the window and when it fell slanting across her throat and cheek, she woke. I don't believe it, she thought, sun, really sun, hot sun, sun like any other place. She sat up, warm, and looked around her room that was bright with a bluish white light thrown back from the snow. Outside the sky was cloudless and water-blue and there was no noise anywhere. It's a miracle, she said to herself, they have sun in Finland. How absolutely lovely everything is. Instead of being a nightmare of cold and grimness, the winter would be lovely. I will ski every day and come back at tea time to my own house. Perhaps they have modern houses like this place; I must find out at once. And Lahti.

She looked at the travelling clock on the bedside table and saw that it was two o'clock and she wondered whether Benno would think there was anything strange about her sleeping so late. No, certainly not; she had been worn-out yesterday, she had a right to sleep into the afternoon. But we were going to the field. I must hurry, we can still go. Lahti will be there now; it is even better. Oh lovely, she said to herself, lovely, lovely, lovely, what a sun.

She listed her plans as she bathed. See him first of all, just see him. Then Helsinki and write the articles; but I must arrange to rent a house before I leave here. I can buy a victrola and a radio and china and vases and lamps and things while I am in Helsinki and bring them back with me. Surely they will have a good modern house near here; they have them everywhere. How shall I word it: "Cannot leave now Charles you will understand. Must stay here and do what I can"? Later, I will write and tell him more. Better just brush out my hair and let it curl any way. All I needed was the sleep and some sun again. I feel wonderful and hungry and how will Lahti look at me, what will his eyes be like? Not like last night because this was morning and it had to be different. Gentle, she thought, and having the secret with me. She stood in the sun and brushed her hair and thought of his face, of his body and all she remembered and she held the brush loosely in her hand and felt herself again without strength, yielding and wanting. Not now, she thought, not now: there will be every day to remember and then waiting for him every night. I must see him now at once before we go to Helsinki. Three days is a lot of time.

Benno and Carl were alone in the great room. The fire was made but unlit and sun came in wide stripes through each of the windows. Carl sat with his back to the sun and the blinding snow and smoked a cigar. Benno stood by the window. They did not talk: the whole house seemed empty. Then they heard the woman's steps coming along the upper hall. They had been waiting for her.

"Good morning," she said, from the door.

Carl looked up quickly. Well there it is, he thought, as I imagined.

"We were waiting for you," Benno said.

"I'm so sorry to keep you waiting. I was dead tired. You really should have waked me. But I have had a grand rest. Do you think I could get some coffee before we go over to the field?"

"We better get back to Helsinki," Benno said.

"Oh Benno, there's no reason to be stuffy about it. We aren't running on a timetable. We have plenty of time to make a quick trip to the field. Colonel Sala gave his permission. Where is Colonel Sala?"

"Working," Carl said. "They work sometime."

What is the matter with them, she thought, and why didn't they wake me if it makes them so cross to be delayed.

"Why didn't you wake me?" she said.

"We thought it better to let you sleep."

"Please order some coffee then, and we'll go."

"I have something to tell you, Mrs. Maynard."

"All right." He can't talk about anything without making it into a mystery or a disaster, she thought. Probably Carl's car has a puncture or the attack isn't going too well around Suomussalmi.

"I do not want to shock you. Perhaps we should wait

until you have had your coffee." You could see he was enjoying it. You could see how he was waiting and tasting it all in advance. But I know you my little man, she thought, I heard you running down the stairs in Viipuri: nothing about you impresses me, neither your mysteries nor your disasters.

"Tell her," Carl said suddenly, in a loud angry voice.

"Will you let me handle this, Petersen?" Benno said smoothly. "I think I am the best one to decide."

"Colonel Sala begs you to excuse him that he is not here to tell you good-by," Benno said.

Carl said one word in Finnish, a short furious word that meant the same thing in any language. He ground out his cigar so that the pewter ashtray rattled on the table and then he walked across the room as if he were crushing rock with his boots and they heard the front door slam behind him, slamming so hard that the noise shook back against the windows.

"He is upset," Benno said, with something like pleasure.

"What is it, Benno? Just tell me whatever it is and let's get started."

"There has been an accident."

"Well?" She was used to Benno, to Benno's false alarms, to Benno's cowardice which exaggerated and made dramatic and terrible the most simple risks or happenings. "Go on."

"This morning."

"But naturally." I'll scream at him, she thought, I'll

throw the ashtrays at him. When would it have happened, if not this morning?

"It was a very bad accident and it happened during the morning patrol."

No, she said to herself. No. This is just Benno, this is the fool Benno, this is the talky-man Benno. You do not have to pay any attention to him. Benno watched her face, carefully, to see how it would take her.

"A plane came down."

"Tell me." Her voice rose, almost shouting at him. You are doing this for fun, you are doing this like sticking pins into flies. "You tell me," she said.

He wished now that he had sent a note up to her room or that one of the officers were here to do this. It was going to be unpleasant and in some way he was afraid for himself. He did not see what she could do to him but he was afraid of her. He had never seen a woman look like this, so hating, with her mouth so hard and so dangerous.

He had planned how to tell her. It was going to be simple, mourning, and she would understand that no Finn felt any sacrifice was too great for his country. He would spare her all shocking details and he would be there to support her.

Now he talked fast, breathlessly, and he was in a hurry to finish but he did not dare to stop.

"It was Lahti. You do not know very much about aviation or combat fighting. The Russian bombers do not come with pursuit planes. Our men go up, not in formation, and attack the Russian bombers singly. This is the way it is always done. There is nothing unusual about it. They have been very successful. Our pursuit is faster, more maneuverable at great altitudes, and the foggy weather has been a help. Today it was very clear, with almost no cover in the clouds. The plane burned as it fell. Maybe he was killed first. One of his squadron reported it when he came back. Sala went over to where they thought it was, Sala and a doctor and all that would be needed. They found him. But there was nothing much left. Of course you see how it would be, with the plane burning. They think perhaps he got a machine-gun bullet before the plane fell. It was very good this morning, very clear. There was not much cover in the clouds. He was alone against five bombers. That is nothing unusual. There have only been two losses here so far. They care very much for Lahti as a man and he is a great pilot. It is a serious loss. It makes a great difference. They do not want any one over at the field. Sala said just to go back to Helsinki. Sala has some arrangements to make at the field, about replacing Lahti. They will bury him near here, I think."

"Oh, stop," she said, *"Stop Stop Stop!"*

She had been watching his mouth. She heard it all, though now she could not remember the words. She knew what he had said. She knew it at once and all the time he talked she stood near him, with her shoulders bent, and listened. The order and the shape were gone from her face. She listened with a slipped stupid unhearing look and then suddenly she seemed to narrow and tower and she cried out at him, and her face closed up, but not as if she were going to cry, it pulled together with horror and she looked once at Benno, as if he were the horrible thing, he the living one, and then she ran out of the room. He heard her running up the stairs.

Benno sat in the chair Carl had left. He would wait here. If she did not come down in half an hour, he would go after her. The others would not want to find Mrs. Maynard when they came back. He could understand that they would not want a woman around. All the officers had been distant and strange, after the news came. It was as if they had never met Benno and Carl before. They seemed to forget yesterday, the meals and the talk together. Colonel Sala was not even very courteous. He had not shaken hands to say good-by. He simply gave orders: "Your car will be ready and filled with petrol. Take Mrs. Maynard directly back to Helsikki." He left no message of good-by for her; that was Benno's own invention. None of the other officers mentioned Mrs. Maynard, or spoke to Carl or Benno, or said good-by or offered to shake hands. They went out of the building as if they had important work to do. They did not even speak together.

Carl did not know that it was always this way. It was the first time he had ever been around when casualties were announced. He did not recognize, as you recognize and accept, the hatred soldiers have for civilians when they hear of a comrade's death. The anger and the bitterness and the pain turn against the civilian who is not dead, and is probably not going to die. The hatred passes, but it is always there when first the casualties are announced. Carl had not seen this before but he felt it, he felt himself ashamed, and he told Benno it would be better if they went to their rooms and left the officers alone. Benno did not go and he resented orders from Carl and said so. Carl stayed in his room until the house was quiet and he knew the officers had gone.

As for Carl, Benno thought, he would make a report to the Propaganda Ministry about Carl. Carl did not seem to realize that he was only a sort of chauffeur. He would call Mrs. Maynard in another half hour. Colonel Sala had certainly not behaved with courtesy but his meaning was clear.

She crossed the room to the bed, ready to throw herself down on it and lie still and hope it was not true. But she looked at the bed and suddenly it was terrifying to her. It was not this bed, it had not been this bed. Burned, she thought, burned. You could not think about it. You could not think about it any way. He was so tall, but not foolish the way very tall men are because all of him fitted together. He moved in one piece, without any noise. He never made an extra gesture. No one had those eyes, the wonderful carved nose, the tight close-cut stiff hair. How did he look then, after falling from that height, and burned? It did not happen. It was some one else. No, it did happen. No.

She walked about the room, walking very fast from the window to the far wall. Then she realized what she was doing and she sat down in a chair and the light from the windows hurt her eyes and she turned the chair so that it faced the wall. Then she sat straight in the chair and began saying it over to herself; it did not happen. What did not happen? He did not fall, he did not, he did not come down burned. Burned and mashed, her mind insisted. It did not happen last night then; then it did not happen last night. Then there was no one last night. Then that was it. There was nothing last night. I was never going to stay here. I am going back to London of course. There was no other thing. If it did not happen last night, it did not happen today.

I do not know anybody who dies. I saw them in Helsinki. They were like old rags; they were torn up. They were pitiful but they were not people you know. It always happens in a war but it is some one in the street or some one in a hospital. You write about it. It is terrible. But it is not some one of yours. Not to any one you know. Not to the one who last night. There was no last night then. But if it could happen, if there was a last night and if you could remember his hands, his weight, his warmth, the wildness, the owning, the black dark soft lost melting

118

ending, then if there was today, and burned and falling from a great height and burned, then it could happen to some one who was yours. It could happen to you. The torn-up rags on the street could be you too, now. The torn-up rags could have a name. Some one could come and say: I will identify her. Some one went to look at the burned one and said: this is he. It could happen to you, it *could* happen.

I knew it, she told herself, I did know it. I knew when they bombed Helsinki: I knew about pursuit pilots. I did. No I didn't, she thought wildly, I didn't, I didn't. No one of mine.

She stood up and looked around the room. This morning, waking with all the plans and the lovely sun, was gone. That was some one else. That was not true. She picked up her clothes and put them in the bag; she collected the soap and toothbrush, the gold-backed comb and brush, the specially prepared pefume from the bathroom and kneeled on the suitcase to shut it. Where is my coat? she thought, we must go now. We must go quickly. If you think about it, it will happen to you too; you must stay away from it, you must not be part of it, you must not admit it.

Then she had her suitcase in her hand, and standing by the door she remembered, so that she could not deny it, how she waited with her ski boots, listening for him. But I loved him, she thought. I needed him. It was going to be so perfect. It was what I always wanted, it was what I was always waiting for. And now I have nothing. It is far worse than if I had never seen him.

"No," she said aloud, standing by the door, "it isn't fair. It can't be this way."

Benno heard her and went to meet her at the foot of the stairs. When he saw that she was carrying her suitcase he went up to take it from her. She was crying. He was glad to see that she was crying softly, letting the tears streak down her cheeks but not making any noise about it. She followed him through the door and out to the car. She opened the front door, though Benno was standing ready to help her into the back. She got in by Carl. Benno wrapped the blankets around her and climbed in to sit alone, putting her suitcase on the seat beside him. Carl turned the car and none of them looked back at the great handsome white building.

And now I will never have anything, she thought. She held her head bowed, and from time to time she wiped her eyes but she was not thinking of how she looked and she had forgotten Carl and Benno. It is just gone like that, for no reason, she thought. There is no reason. Why did he have to do it, why do any of them have to do it? We could have had everything and now it is all gone. But how did he look, she thought, and she stopped crying and held herself stiff, with a choked dizzy nausea coming over her. Then she was not thinking at all, but only keeping her mind empty so that she would not guess how he had been when they found him and the burned crushed plane.

Her face is green, Carl thought, I better give her a drink.

"Take some aquavit," he said. He squirmed around so that he could get his hand inside his coat. He offered her the bottle but she shook her head.

"I'll have some myself then." He did not pass the bottle back to Benno. He did not want to speak to Benno at all, not even to say: have a drink. He could not forget Benno, making himself important with the news of Lahti's death. Benno is a dishonor, Carl thought gravely.

She watched the road and the bare snow fields; keeping her eyes open and watching so as not to think. But she could not stop it. Some one of yours. It can happen to you too. I will cable Charles to meet me in London. I do not want to be alone, I cannot be alone. Do not be a part of it, do not belong in it, do not understand it: there is no reason for such a thing, but it can happen to any one now, without reason.

Then she was crying again, not trying to hide it or quiet it. Her body trembled and she found it hard to breathe and she could see nothing. She hunched her shoulders together and wept. I have lost everything I wanted, senselessly, cruelly, uselessly, without a reason. And there was this nearness now, this terrible nearness, it was close to you all the time, it could happen to any one, it could happen to you.

Carl was cramped in the little car, and the steering

wheel held him like a belt, and his coat was bulky and he needed both hands; the road was very bad here. But he moved himself awkwardly to pat her shoulder and he said, "Don't cry." In a way, he was glad she was crying. There was nothing he could do: but she could cry. Lahti was a fine man, a fine man of this country and a great pilot and Finland was losing them every day, the fine ones, the good and the brave, the skilled ones who were needed all the time, in war and in peace.

"It's so horrible," she said, choking on the words. Her voice was muffled in her handkerchief. "I can't help it. It's so horrible for me."

"What is?" he said. He did not understand. He thought she was crying for Lahti.

"This war," she said.

Carl turned and looked at her. He was driving very slowly because of the road and he took a chance for a moment and turned so that he could see her face. He felt he would want to know about her face. He would want to know how such a face could possibly be. But she was hidden by the fur hood and the handkerchief and he could see nothing.

"You don't mean it," he said heavily. "You don't really mean it."

Perhaps he would have better luck on his next job. Perhaps they would send him out with better people.

Zoo in Madrid

WE WERE sick of the war. We had no right to be since we were not the men in the trenches nor were we the blind American in the hospital at Salices nor the little Spaniard in the first-aid post near Jarama, who had no arm. We were not even especially hungry. But it was such fine weather and we knew it was spring everywhere else and probably spring here too, if you could only see it. The guns near Carabanchel were taking the day off and we wanted to have a good time, something not exciting or important or grave or memorable but just fun.

We walked down the Prado, up behind the museum, and came to the first carved iron gate which opens into the Parque de Madrid. A man was vaguely selling shoestrings in front of the gate, four children were climbing on it and it was locked. It had been locked, so they said, ever since the war started. Behind the gate you could see the new green trees and instead of grass there were banks of shiny small green leaves with little blue flowers scattered through them. Inside we knew it would be even better.

We walked down to the next gate and spoke to the

sentry. We said, "We are North American journalists and we have been visiting all the fronts and now we would like to see what is beautiful in Spain." He understood that. He called a friend of his, a little man with a coffee-colored soft shrivelled face and a voice like a penny whistle, who was also a guard. The first guard repeated what we had said and his friend scratched his head and said, there are the orders. . . .

"Yes," we said encouragingly, and all four of us waited in the sun.

"It is a very beautiful park," we said, "you can see even from here."

That fixed it. We followed the little coffee-colored guard across the sandy paths. We passed a sunken garden, ornate with twisting hedges, old foolish statues of armored heroes in fine attitudes, and some fountains of which one had been smashed by a shell. You made a crunching noise in the sand as you walked which is one of the best things to listen to in the world, there were no guns going at all and there were birds somewhere.

The little guard said that the high delicate tree with purple blossoms on it was called the tree of love. There were white pointed starflowers in the grass, the petals veined with green. There were flowering horse-chestnuts and laurels and lilacs and the soft warm wet green smell that means spring.

The guard led us to the lake, a what you call ornamental piece of water, with a huge monument at one end.

This monument begins with sea-nymphs and conch-shells and lions at the bottom and on the very top is a solid figure—Alfonso XII—astride a solid horse. Between the conch-shells and the King there is a heavy double semi-circle of granite pillars but these are messed up now because a shell hit here too. It seems that in December, right behind two lions and a nymph, there was a gun position and the Fascists sent a shell back to it in greeting.

You could see very small fishes in the lake but the big fishes had died some time ago because they had to drain the lake. It reflected moonlight and when the enemy planes came over at night it was a guide to them, showing them the center of Madrid.

So we stood and enjoyed the lake and the air and the new green trees and the guard was very pleased that we had come all the way from North America to appreciate this fine Spanish park.

He took us to the park guardian who had offices in the Jardin Botanico and as we were already there they decided to show us the zoo. It is a very sweet zoo, intimate and absurd, with little cage-houses hopefully imitating the architecture of the original country of the animals. The elephant lives in an odd-looking sort of Hindu temple; the monkeys are in a thatched affair which may or may not be somewhat like an African village hut; the peacocks are housed in tile. A large rhododendron bush blooms red in the midst of this and dozens of smooth white pigeons make a steady soft noise which is very far away from war.

The zoo was tidily kept, as were the park grounds. Men who had worked in the Casa de Campo where a big attack is now going on, or in the Parque del Oueste which is laced with trenches, were transferred here and they continue to shape the hedges and weed and rake the paths and when they must they cut the trees, or just the tops of the trees, for firewood for the hospitals.

Five guards had gathered around us now, all pleased to show the zoo, and we told them how handsome the baby llama was and what a superb great yak they had here and as we became more involved in the wonders of the zoo and closer friends they said they would consider it an honor to show us the hippopotamus. We said we would love to see the hippopotamus. (Is there really a war going on, or what is this? One of the guards picked two camellias, one white and one red, and gave them to me. A little boy appeared from nowhere on a bicycle and followed us from animal to animal, staring. There is of course a war going on, far down the street, where you can see the beginning of the smooth green hills.)

We admired the hippopotamus and we admired also four microscopic new rabbits in the cage next door and then we said we were grateful for this privilege and we would have to go.

We shook hands with every one and said *salud* and made a few more compliments on the zoo and then the little guard walked back with us. Walking slowly, we began to talk about the war. We did not think any one would

126

believe us when we got home, or understand, or even care. They would not know, we decided, how important this war was because it was like nothing else before it.

We said to each other the things we already knew by heart: that we had never in one place seen people so different, so real, and so disinterested. That was the first thing and perhaps the biggest. Then we began to talk about how incredible it was to have everything mixed up together, the zoo and the gun positions behind the statue, and the café that grew up in one half of a shelled building: on one side of the first floor is chaos, chairs hanging on a chandelier, an iron stove that was hurled down through the floor into the center of a former cabaret, cracked mirrors and the usual inevitable masses of waste paper. They built a flimsy partition, to shut out this mess, and there is the café doing business as usual. We talked of the way the people of Madrid take what comes with a serenity that passes belief and we talked of boys in the trenches who had had twelve hours of military training and got further lessons in the midst of an attack. I told about the coiffeur's shop where four women were having permanent waves when a shell struck two floors above and no one moved. Rabb told me about standing in the fifth floor of a half-destroyed house, watching an attack in the Casa de Campo, through field glasses, and then a shell hit the house. They moved to another floor and shaded their glasses and after awhile they came back to the first place because the view was better. In that house you sit and watch the trenches and watch an arc of smoke rise from a shelled hill and it is only ten minutes' walk from where you live. In what was once the dining room, the china is miraculously intact in neat piles and there are pictures of the disappeared owners as a very stiff bride and groom.

So we came to the park gate, full of wonder for this war and admiring the people who were in it, and the guard said he was enchanted to have met us and we said we were too and that we hoped we would meet again.

By this time we were in a splendid humor: the situation evidently called for beer. We decided on Chicote's. Going down a side street toward the Prado we heard the first shell. The sound came from the direction of the Gran Via and from here it made a noise like blasting in a quarry. When shells sound like that you feel interested but safe; it is when you hear the whistle-scream-roar that you wish you were some place farther away. We heard the second, closer. The streets were full of people taking their pre-dinner stroll. We hurried because we wanted to see what had happened.

Just a little way down from Chicote's on the Gran Via we saw a wide new hole, the granite cobblestones lying smashed and dusty around it, and leading to the nearest doorway was a neat straight fresh trail of blood. Chicote's was crowded with soldiers and civilians and handsome Spanish girls with peroxided hair. The beer was cold and good.

November Afternoon

THE THREE biggest barges on this piece of the Loing Canal were called Jo-Bert, Odessa and Azur. In the stern by the long rudder handle were pots of chrysanthemums because the barge women always kept the land with them somehow. Washing hung on wire cords, stretched the whole great length of the boats. The men steered the barges up from the river into the locks and on each barge a woman stood in the darkening afternoon and the rainy wind, beside her man, and watched him guide their barge through the water. Some barges were tied up in the river against the shore. One barge carried its tow horse aboard and you saw, walking along the path, the open stall and the shining chestnut rump of the horse. There was a fine land smell of hay near that boat. Some old men were talking to each other by the shore plank of a tug. It would be night in another hour, at five o'clock, and the boats and barges were coming in to tie up until morning.

Everybody seemed very much at home. The people on

the barges lived on their boats as firmly as if these were houses in the suburbs of Lyons or Nancy. The small cafés and shops which sold fishing tackle and rope and kerosene and canned goods, beside the canal, were old and unchanging: the proprietors did not move away to bigger trade and better stores, the clientele came in regularly from the rivers, always the same, and did their business year after year spending neither more money nor less. It was a gray and rose afternoon, soft with rain, and along the Loing the trees held their last yellow leaves. The canal and the river were beautiful because they were quiet and gentle and also because people worked here without anxiety.

The woman said, "They have a fine life on the barges. They're settled."

The man was walking ahead of her, making a slurring sound in the dead leaves of the river path. He did not hear or just did not answer. He stopped by a thin middle-aged man who wore a blue denim workman's suit and black wooden shoes.

"What are you fishing?" he asked softly, so as not to disturb anything.

"*Brochet,*" the fisherman said. The man stood a moment, admiring the three round red floats that kept the line up on the water. The river was wide and gray-green and opposite was a small shack with a vegetable garden and a light in the front windows. It was a river that made you homesick not for any place but just to be growing

beside it, the way the other people were, tying up a
barge or steering it, fishing, or watering the chrysanthemums.

The woman walked up and waited beside the man.
"He's liable to get a big brochet too," the man said.

"Doesn't it smell lovely," the woman said, "the water
smell and the leaves?"

"Yes."

She walked on; the path was narrow and he walked
faster than she, away from her. He had his own thoughts
and he needed time, not to think them out but to feel
all around them and recognize them and put them in
their proper places. The woman was suddenly hurt like
touching a bruised place, a light quick hurt. She walked
after him but she did not hurry: she made herself alone
with the river and the golden drooping trees and the
smell of the damp earth and the water.

People like us, she thought, walking slowly along the
river, I'm sick of people like us. We have all the dressy
unreal problems of the rich. The problems I like, she told
herself, are whether it's going to rain or whether you
really will catch a brochet or whether the washing will
dry by morning or whether you're bringing the barge in
straight to the locks or whether you'll get the cargo to
Havre on time. Such things. Good solid problems that
you can think about and then there they are, settled one
way or another. I'm sick of myself, she thought with
passion, me and my heart.

She scuffed her feet, making the leaves rub together dryly and sharply; she hoped he would turn around and wait for her and take her arm. She hoped they could just walk along the river path as simple and free as any girl from Moret, out on a Sunday afternoon with her sweetheart. He was walking with his shoulders high, looking ahead of him up the river. Her hurt turned into anger.

Why can't we be happy, she thought, happy or contented like decent people? What are all these bloody things that people like us invent to spoil our lives. She was not blind to her anger or to the injustice of it but she felt it coming over her and she would not stop it.

"We'll cross here," he said, though she had not noticed that he was waiting, "and go back to the car down the other side." He helped her up the cement steps of the viaduct and they walked behind each other, alongside the great oil tube on the narrow footbridge. He waited at the foot of the stairs on the other side to see that she got down safely and then he set out again ahead of her. Trees grew close to the water on this side of the river and closed over the path. The leaves were deep and soft with damp. They walked quietly. She had not spoken to him on the bridge and she did not try again. She let him get ahead of her and stayed behind, feeling her anger grow.

"It's not my fault," she thought, and was shocked to hear such words in her head. He won't let us be happy, he won't let us be quiet and settled, he won't let us make a life. And what have we got anyhow? We can't even walk along a river and be happy. We've got to carry our damned miseries with us wherever we go. And we haven't a right to miseries, it's stupid, that's what it is. It's ungrateful. People like us. It's maddening, she thought, and was suddenly surprised that her voice had not broken out under the trees in the evening quiet, sharp and irritable, even whining.

She looked up and saw him ahead; the dark round back of his head, the shoulders held high and tight, the way he walked on his toes lightly. She looked away. She did not want to notice him or think about him; if she did it would come back. She would feel hurt and helpless and weak with pity for him. The pity, she thought, that you have for a sick animal or a sick child, a responsible aching pity. The anger was warm and gave her strength: with anger, you could fight. The worst of all was to go through the days painfully hoping everything would turn out all right in the end.

Even if he has to leave, she thought, he could be happy while we're together. If he loved me, that would be enough. He wouldn't always be worrying about other people and other places. This would be enough while we have it.

"Be careful of the ropes," he said. They were back at the canal and the mooring ropes from the barges stretched taut over the ground, the same color as the leaves. It was getting dark.

Let him leave, she told herself. If you can't be happy

today, you aren't going to be happy on Thursday. All
right, I'm a failure. I can't make him happy. Let him go
back to where he came from. Anything is better than
this. . . . But somewhere in her mind, beside the anger,
quiet and deep was the fear: and what will you do when
he is gone? What will you do, my brave: what will you
do when he is gone? What will you do, my brave: eat
your anger, go bright and angry through the days?

"I hate winter," she said suddenly to the darkness ahead.
Her voice was so cold, so stiff that he turned around.

"Do you?" he said wonderingly. He had been thinking
of many things but not of winter. He had been trying to
see a clean way out of their trouble. But he was tired and
not used to trouble and he had a feeling that every one
was pulling at him, hammering on him, arguing, whispering, bullying, hurrying. He had also begun to think
that he would like a few things for himself, that it would
be good at last not always to consider his actions as they
affected others. He thought it would be fine just to do
something he wanted to do and the hell with all the people who could be hurt or disappointed.

Like strangers, she said to herself, bitterly and with
loneliness. Like a pair of wretched strangers.

The car shone in the darkness. He climbed in and
turned on the lights and the houses beside the tow path
stood out flatly against the trees, with the water flat in
front of them. Sitting still in the car she felt warm from

the walk and comfortably tired. Everything's fine, she thought, except us.

"What do you want to do?" she said.

He said, "Go home." He had not meant it any special way, he just thought it would be nice to go back to Paris now, to a hotel that they were used to and have a drink and dinner on a tray and read. But it sounded to her like saying what's the difference where we go, as we're not going to have any fun about it anyhow, we may as well go home. It sounded to her like weariness and defeat and she sat in the darkness with her hands clenched, hating him and herself and the way they were using their lives.

"I thought we were going to spend the weekend in the country," she said.

"We still can," he said nicely, "but we didn't see any very good places, did we? And we know the hotel's good in Paris. We can always drive out again tomorrow afternoon and walk. There's so little time left that it seems silly to try to get settled in some dreary place, just for a night or two."

"All right," she said.

"No," he said, "we'll stay in the country. Even if we have to sleep out of doors."

"We will not," she said, her voice cruel and hating. "We'll go back to Paris. I wouldn't stay in the country for anything. We'll go back to Paris and get through the week as best as we can, the way we do nowadays, gloomy and businesslike. And then you'll leave. That's what we'll do."

"You're working something up," he said, warily. "And it's going to be my fault that we haven't had a fine week-end in the country before I go. But there isn't any decent hotel, you saw yourself."

Now it was on her like fever or drunkenness. She knew it and she knew how bad it would be and she knew it was wrong. But the words were ready in her mouth, without thought, and she said them:

"I'm not angry or hurt or anything," she said in a false voice, holding her breath.

"What are you then?" he said.

"I just think our life together is a bore," she said, and suddenly thought, you couldn't have revenged yourself better could you, you horror, you couldn't have found a better revenge.

"What do you mean?" he said.

But she could not do anything more about it, she could not explain or take it back or do anything about it. It was done. If he had been angry too they would have fought it out, harsh and quick, and beaten each other into life and awareness. She could then perhaps have found him again and brought him near to her: out of anger she could perhaps have salvaged these last days that remained.

But her anger was gone, with the cruelty.

"I thought our life was many things," he said, "but not

that. It wouldn't be possible you could have used the wrong word?"

She laughed: but he would never know why and it had happened as fast as breathing. She laughed with pride in him, in his kindness against her cruelty and with pleasure in his voice that had been the voice of some one very young and very gentle. But the laugh shook wrong at the end.

He waited a moment as if he could not believe it. Then he started the car. He drove well and fast through the cramped paved village streets and fast on the ugly wide highway to Paris. He did not talk any more. She sat far away from him and he was entirely alone. He did not notice the night or the speed or the names of the towns they passed. He drove the car from habit, back to Paris because you had to drive a car somewhere.

She felt the wind catching her hair and twisting it straight up about her head. The road was very long but that did not matter. She was in no hurry to arrive any place. I've sent him away, she thought, now he's really gone. I sent him away. Before, he was just going to leave but now I've sent him away. The anger was all gone but the fear settled in her like a sickness, like a long deep sickness that you could never find the cure for. The wind was cold on her face and she thought that in November you begin to know how long the winter will be.

A Sense of Direction

THE ITALIAN COMMANDANTE was not as handsome as everybody said he was. There was a new tight up-curve of stomach beginning at the second button of his trousers; the skin of his cheeks was loosening and the pores were large. In mixed company he wore a lustrous expression, his teeth, his eyes and his smile all shining. You could see that he had been saying successful things to women all his life.

He had been an exile from Italy for five years but he was very patriotic and conscious of being an Italian and Caporetto was never mentioned in front of him. He did not catch on to jokes very well but he was extremely brave. His men loved him and the Brigade officers would tell you admiring and affectionate stories about him and they did not mind his being a romantic hero, though romantic heroes were not exactly the style of this war. He had a great talent for soldiering and his Battalion was already famous.

That week the German batteries on Garabitas hill had

been shelling Madrid three or four times a day. The weather was beautiful and in the daytime the shellings were usually fast and short, sixty shells in twelve minutes, and the bombardment was concentrated on the center of town from the Cibeles monument down to the Puerta del Sol. In the daytime people got out of the way as best they could and waited and went on with their business or pleasure. But at night the shellings were heavier and lasted longer and the shells swept recklessly over the city and people could not sleep. The food was scarce of course, and a diet of codfish and never getting enough sleep was making us all a little short tempered. We were anxious to get out in the country at least during the day and we welcomed any invitations to staff headquarters or the front because the weather was fine, the fronts were restful after Madrid, and the army had plenty of food. At some staff headquarters you were even offered American cigarettes. There had been nothing to write about for weeks since no one anywhere was interested in another shelling of Madrid.

I came back to the hotel at three after an unsuccessful attempt to buy soap and the concierge told me that the comrade journalists were all out. Don Federico had taken the Señorita Bourke (pronounced Boorque) with him. Where did they go? They went past the Montana Barracks to the street that overlooked the Casa de Campo because they had heard much machine-gun fire from that direction and thought there might be something to see.

(With glasses you could follow the action very well if there was any action. We had a deserted half-house out there, whose fourth floor was practically intact, which we used as a grandstand for the Casa de Campo trenches.) Where was Thompson? Tomsohn had gone out to buy victrola records; Luis (Bob Lewis) had been looking for me because he was going over to call on our friends in Userra, the 36th Brigade who lived like moles in their wonderful deep complicated trenches dug among the stumps of houses in that suburb.

The Plaza del Callao was lined with people waiting to see Ken Maynard and his Wonder Horse, in the movie palace across the street, and a peddler came through pushing a handcart full of oranges, with a stream of women holding on to each other so as not to lose their places, pursuing him like a game of follow-the-leader; and the concierge said wistfully that it was a day for a peekneek and he regretted to see me abandoned and bored. It doesn't matter, I said, I have some work to do, which I hadn't, and I went up to my room thinking that Fred Lawrence might at least have waited for me and taken me with Liz Bourke or just have waited for me.

The concierge telephoned ten minutes later and said that the chauffeur of the Italian Commandante was downstairs with an invitation from the Commandante to come out to the front and have supper. I would be ready at once, I said, and put my last two packages of cigarettes in my coat pocket. I was very pleased. The Commandante had a low opinion of civilians and had never, as far as I knew, sent his car into town for any one before. Besides, I thought greedily, hurrying down the stairs, there will be meat for dinner.

It would not have been proper to ask either the chauffeur or the soldier with him where we were going. I saw that we were making a wide circle around University City out to Cuatro Caminos. Then we turned left on rutted and dusty roads and bumped over low hills and you smelled the sun and the land was very open and silent. It seemed far away from Madrid but it could not have been. You could hear a sparse bombardment going on, the shells whirred into the distance and did not disturb the sleepiness and warmth of the country. The car crashed in and out of a shell hole and I thought of the springs and thought it was incredible that no one seemed able to drive sensibly in this country and now the road ran downhill through short trees and we stopped off the road in the shade and the chauffeur and the soldier got out and began covering the car with loose branches to hide it better and then the three of us sat on the running board and waited.

I offered them cigarettes which they took with many nods and sounds of pleasure and they both held the cigarettes up to admire them: real cigarettes rolled in a factory, whole and unsmoked, Americano moreover. They lit them and looked at the cigarettes between puffs.

"The Commandante will come for you here," the chauffeur said.

"Good."

"Much bombardment in Madrid?" the soldier asked.

"Mucho."

"Much fear?" he asked, smiling.

I don't know how it is in a war with Anglo-Saxons. I suppose one would always say wryly: boy, was I scared. I imagine that would be the fashion though I do not know. But with Spaniards the thing is to be dauntless. With simple Spaniards one can be as heroic as possible, they enjoy it and do not believe it necessarily but it is a manner of speaking which pleases. With complicated Spaniards it is well to be dignified and silent, ignoring even the thought of fear.

So I said: "Man, the people of Madrid are without fear as all the world knows." In fact the people of Madrid had to be without fear, for practical purposes, and in fact the people of Madrid were without fear as far as one could see.

Both the chauffeur and the soldier were Madrileños, and that answer was a good one. They put on serious expressions and nodded in approval.

"And you yourself," the soldier said. He was a tease, I could see that. I did not know what was the best thing to say. I could have told him a wonderful story about that same morning and the ten o'clock bombardment during which the hotel was hit three times. Liz Bourke came down to my room just before the shelling started because I had some instant coffee powder and an electric heater to boil water and in the mornings I was quite popu-

lar with people dropping in for a cup of that bitter hot
unsatisfactory stuff. We were drinking this pseudo-coffee
when the shelling started and we talked louder and louder
above the noise. Liz was telling me how all her pals at
Biarritz had warned her before she came, explaining that
she was crazy, it was very dangerous in Spain, she would
be killed. Then there would be a sharpening high
stretched scream as a shell passed to hit farther behind us
up the Gran Via. Liz would stop a moment while the
noise was worst and then go on. "Such nonsense," she
said, "I've never felt cosier in my life." I was listening
carefully for the shells. Then the hotel was hit for the
third time, somewhere up above, and there was a sort of
thudding rock and the tinkle of glass. I noted that. Liz
said, "I want to ask you something." I prepared to be
cordial but uncommunicative. She said, "I want to know,
darling, what *is* communism?" It had been a fairly bad
shelling and I laughed a little too much and said I had
never been able to understand the literature but I supposed
she should read Marx, Engels and Lenin and she would
no doubt find the answer and then I had to visit a hospital
so I left her.

It was too difficult to tell that story in Spanish and perhaps it would not have answered the soldier's question,
so I said, *"Regulár."*

He laughed. *"Regulár,"* he said, "Good."

The chauffeur stood up; then the soldier and I got up
too and I walked down the road. The Commandante was

143

coming towards us. He looked thinner, handsome and very gay. He took off his cap while he was still some distance away and the sun made his hair steely and bright. His hair was the same color as his skin, grayish; but his skin was not sick looking, it was the colorless tough kind that could not be browned by sun or reddened by cold. His hair was crisp and well-cut and he had shaved and he wore a red handkerchief around his neck. No uniforms were alike at this time and the Commandante seemed to be elegantly dressed for ski-ing, in a brown outfit with the red scarf added because of visitors.

He spoke French with a flat metallic accent and I thanked him very much for letting me come out. I noticed the soldier and chauffeur who were standing a little to the left. They both smiled at the Commandante in a special way. I had thought the Commandante was doing me a professional kindness, giving me a chance for a story, only a small story probably but anything was better than re-writing the Madrid shellings. The Commandante gave his orders in a mixture of Italian and Spanish. They were to return with the car near the bridge at ten o'clock. They saluted and left us; you could not hear what they were saying as they walked back towards the car but they were laughing together.

"You are ready?" the Commandante said. "You feel yourself brave?"

I followed him along a path that grew narrower and sloped easily down the side of the hill. I could hear the river but not see it through the trees. It would be the Manzanares.

"Where are we?" I said.

"We are far along at the edge of the Parque del Oeste."

It was sweet country, as quiet as the south of France, with pine trees growing from the sandy soil and laurel bushes and aspen only turning green now because the spring was late. The fallen pine needles were slippery to walk on and the air smelled as nothing had smelled for a long time. The sky was a smooth polished blue dappled with puff clouds. I was homesick for country like this, lovely gentle and quiet country, and for a quiet unimportant life where you had all the time you wanted to breathe and lie on your back watching the sky, where nothing tragic or harsh happened within your range of vision.

"Are you in a hurry?" the Commandante asked.

There was not a sound; we could have been anywhere except Spain.

"Oh no," I said.

He chose a place where the pine needles were thick and dry and the afternoon sun warmed them to a golden tobacco color. He sat down and lit a cigarette and then stretched out with one arm beneath his head. I stood above him, foolishly.

"Viens," he said, smiling.

Damn, I thought, just when I get some place I really like complications set in.

I sat down, not too close but close enough for politeness.

"You are not friendly," he said, turning his head and his smile. "I have always heard American women were principally intellectual."

Fighting words, I thought, and at that moment the first shell went over. It was from one of our batteries and it seemed to go over low and with a beating of wings and you thought you could see it if you looked hard enough.

"What are we shelling?" I asked. There had been several small attacks in the Casa de Campo earlier in the week, starting with a very limited artillery preparation.

"Something," he answered. "You are interested in the war?"

"Well," I said, "you know I'm a journalist. I earn my living writing. Now here in Spain for instance there is a war so I earn my living trying to write about it. I understand very little but I am learning as much as I can."

"It is a long time since I have had an afternoon on a hillside with a woman."

Of course, I thought, he wouldn't be here if there was any action planned for this sector. Another great heavy bird plowed across the sky. Then there was a rock-splitting boom far away beyond the river.

"It's nice," I said, "as long as they're going out. It makes a nice comfortable sound."

"Look at me," he said and took my hand. "Why do you talk so much?"

"Americans always talk. Haven't you noticed? It's

146

very well known. Americans talk without interruption."

"You do not like me?"

"I like you very much."

"Then come here. And be quiet."

This shell was an incomer. It was far above us and landed far behind, on the road I thought. There was no danger; but there was the sound. I couldn't explain what that sound did to you; how it tightened in your stomach and pressed on your throat, how it made you feel suddenly all alive, violently alive, so that you collected yourself and knew your whole body belonged to you, how it excited you and made you feel a little sick but gay and you could see better than you had a moment ago and hear more. I noticed the shape of the leaves of the laurel bush behind his head and exactly how the shadows fell on his shoulder and right sleeve. The second shell landed closer behind us but still far away.

"War is terrible for a man," the Commandante said with obvious insincerity. I never saw any one who enjoyed war more, who so prospered and flourished in it.

I looked at him and laughed. And suddenly he laughed too.

"Come on," he said, "I will take you to the trenches."

We walked down to the Manzanares. It flowed clear and fast like a trout stream, curving through pale green willows, flowing under a bridge, widening out with sandy flats on either side and then disappearing around another turn. A soldier was washing a khaki shirt under the bridge, and farther up a soldier was fishing. We crossed on stepping stones; the bridge was in range of enemy artillery but the high banks protected us. We walked along the stream to a place where they had cut a trench that led up the bank and along to a smashed farmhouse. All smashed farmhouses have a tendency to look alike, some more ruined than others. We skirted the outside walls, walking in trenches that were shoulder high, stepping over or around the places you would have to avoid and once the Commandante called out to a soldier ahead who quickly pulled his pants up and ran down a communicating trench. The trench was not deep enough and if it rained you would need water wings, I thought, but the weather was fine and I had not seen really deep trenches. I thought either the average height of the Spanish soldier must be inches below my own or else I just had a feeling about walking around like some sort of moving target in a shooting gallery.

A thick stone wall, five feet high, ran at right angles to the farmhouse and mounted the hill. The wall was mostly solid though in places it had been blown open and in other places the top looked as if it had been roughly scalloped. Soldiers sat holding their rifles between their knees in shallow holes they had dug against this wall. The trench was parallel to the wall and about six feet from it. The Commandante, walking ahead of me, looked different. You could see in the soldiers' faces how he looked. Some saluted and some waved at him, some called out:

they all smiled the same way. He seemed to know each one of them (the similar dark unshaved weary faces) and he knew how they loved him. It was more than that though that was rare enough. The line of soldiers changed: it was as if, only seeing him, they felt safe and proud of themselves and they became solidly his Battalion as he walked by: before they had been unidentified men, each one lonely with his rifle, waiting for another day to end.

There were two soldiers in front of us: they walked with their heads well down. The Commandante walked as if we were on the Champs Elysées, taking the afternoon air. I behaved as he did, having the honor of the press to up-hold. Two officers of his staff joined us; they had evidently been hurrying to catch up. They greeted me without enthusiasm.

"Where are you going, Giorgio?" one of them asked. He was older than the Commandante and wore glasses and he looked worried and angry.

"Up ahead."

"It is not necessary."

The Commandante patted his shoulder.

"We must get a steel hat for the lady," the officer said coldly.

The Commandante never wore one.

"Si, si," he said.

The officers followed us, growling to each other. We were strung out about five feet apart.

Then the Commandante stopped and said to me, "The soldiers are pleased to see me taking a woman up here. That way they think the position is good. In fact, it is a very ugly position, a stupid and ugly position. I lost eight men yesterday with head wounds. We are below them and they have those who can handle a rifle. Now here it is bad at this corner, so bend down and run."

This trench was deep enough but it seemed to me a definitely gloomy place. The soldiers looked tired and serious and scarcely noticed us, only flattening themselves against the front wall of the trench to let us pass. They saluted or spoke to the Commandante but in low voices and not wasting time on it. He stopped by a tall fair boy and said, "See, I have brought you a pretty visitor to your trench," and the boy looked at me and smiled quickly and turned away. The Commandante said something to the younger of his staff officers, speaking close to him and fast, but his voice was different too. It was a question or an order and he was answered gravely and he shook his head twice as if he did not like the answer. The trench was wide enough for two to stand together if they almost stood on each other's feet and I waited farther on.

"Do you wish to see?" the Commandante asked.

"Yes."

He took my arm and put me alongside a footsquare opening; a soldier moved away, leaning his rifle against the trench.

"Look in quickly from the side. Your face shows too white. You should be dirtier. Look quickly."

I ducked forward obediently and saw the hill rising rather steeply. It was quieter out there than it had been on the pine needles beyond the river; it was a darker country; the trees looked small and worn out, the land was gray and cold; and it was as if this piece of earth had not kept up with the spring.

"Did you see them?"

"What?"

"Ours."

I looked again longer and saw to the right four things like gray duffle bags strangely placed, half-standing and heavily and unnaturally bent.

"We could not get them in. It is too close."

"Oh," I said. And I thought: they are so dead, so absolutely dead, so far away even from the shape of the living that you can't imagine how they ever looked or what they have lost. You would have to have known their names or known them when they were walking around with the others.

A trench mortar exploded either in the trench or on the parapet farther along the line, to the right. We were standing all together like a bunch of grapes, pressed and overlapping. This is not very smart, I thought.

The older officer said, "Are you spending the night here, Commandante?"

The Commandante had been listening with his head on one side. "Nothing," he said. Then to himself, "What a place. Nothing happens here except senseless accidents."

"Have you seen enough?" he asked me.

I had seen the dead. There were no other sights. The romance of war, I thought, waiting around for head wounds with a view of four gray duffle bags whom you once knew by name.

"Yes, I have seen enough."

He took my hand and pulled me after him. We were walking alone.

"You are sad, little one?"

"Oh no," I said. "It's delightful, isn't it?"

"Whoever said it was?" he asked angrily. "I am losing good men all the time. For nothing."

We passed the evening soup coming up in a caldron carried on a pole by two men who sloshed it over when they ducked to run past the open places and were shouted at by the crouching soldiers in the shallow holes, the soldiers complaining that their dinner was being wasted for them. Two soldiers, like gnomes in a fairy story, went by bowed under big khaki bread sacks. It was getting dark and you found yourself stumbling against the sides of the trench and tripping against rocks you had not noticed in the daytime. A machine gun made a woodpecker sound that was not alarming in the night but rather pleasant and cheerful. A few spent bullets buzzed by like June bugs in the dusk, fast purposeful June bugs, I thought.

"Are you hungry?"

"Very," I said.

We waited for the two officers to join us.

"Alberto," the Commandante said, "go ahead and show us the way."

The officer with glasses laughed. I did not know until later what a big joke it was in the Battalion that the Commandante could never find his way in the dark.

Alberto led us to a little hill behind and above the smashed farmhouse. There were seven officers, two chauffeurs, the cook and two soldiers who did not seem to have any special reason for being there but they handed the tin plates around. We all ate together. One of the officers was a Jugoslav, one a Spaniard and the others Italian. A very uncertain French seemed to be the best language for the greatest number. There were hunks of tender greasy lamb and potatoes in a tomato-flavored stew. The red wine was cold and tasted of the tin cups. The Jugoslav, who was very tall when he got up to pour wine, talked a great deal, sometimes in a French you could not even guess at and he laughed loudly at his own jokes which were not brilliant. The others were easy and quiet, happy to be resting and to be eating hot food. I could not understand the dark Jugoslav boy. Suddenly he got up, shook hands formally with me and muttered something to the others and went down the hill. When we could not hear him any more the Commandante said, "He will be better in a few days."

Alberto explained to me, "His brother died in the Palace Hotel Hospital in Madrid two days ago. From wounds. It was his younger brother. They had no other family. He loved his brother as well as a man might love his bride. It was always something to tease him about."

"Tell us about Madrid," the Commandante said. I had seen many conversations changed like this.

So I told them the news of Madrid, who had been in town, how we had visited the headquarters of the 11th Brigade last week and Ludwig was having a birthday party at the time and Maria came out from Madrid with a real cake and we almost wept to see it and Ivan had grippe and some of the Americans had come in from the Jarama on leave and the shelling had destroyed a good bar off the Gran Via and there was a new kind of whiskey for sale which burned holes in wool if you happened to spill it on yourself. They were easy to amuse. War lasts longer than people can imagine who do not fight it. Each day is forever long and in between action there is nothing to do and nothing much to talk about. You never see anything or have anything to read, there is only the war. People are grateful for any little change in the way of talk. It was an intimate war in those days, we all knew each other and we could gossip contentedly only mentioning first names.

One of the Italian officers practised his English to the

delight of the others. "You like New York . . . you like
Paris . . . you like Madrid . . . I love you . . . have you
see some theatres presently . . . did it become cold lately?
. . ." He had taken lessons at the Berlitz School in Milan
many years ago when he still had a country.

"Do you enjoy the orchestra?" another Italian asked.
"We are very chic here with music at our meals." The
woodpecker and the June bugs, the great birds flying over,
and then from time to time high and pointed, whistling
like a locomotive, a shell would tear into the woods on
the hill behind us.

It was almost still now and the moon rose higher and I
could see them all, sitting in a circle around the iron stew
pot. We wiped the last tomato gravy and the lamb grease
from the tin plates with hunks of bread and you could
hear the comfortable chewing and one man who breathed
as if he had asthma. Then we lit cigarettes and the two
soldiers took the plates away and clattered them, scraping
off any extra food and shoving them dirty into a sack.
They would wash them at the river. One of the chauffeurs
told a story in Spanish about the chauffeur of the General
and how he was unable to dominate a difficulty with his
spark plugs and he repeated the General's remarks and
all the men laughed a great deal. I did not understand the
story very well but I got the point that the General, who
was Hungarian, made some mistakes in his use of obscenities which, if anything, improved the obscenities.

"What time is it, Alberto?" the Commandante asked.

"Quarter to eight."

"We will start then to walk down to the car."

"I will come with you, Commandante," one of the Italians said.

"No."

"I will walk very far ahead."

"I do not need you," the Commandante said, "thank you."

"You remember last week, Giorgio," Alberto said. His voice was sharp again, the way it had been in the trenches.

"I am tired of hearing about it," the Commandante said pleasantly, "and it was an error."

"*Claro,*" the Spaniard said with feeling.

I wondered what this was about.

"It was an error," Alberto said, "which could be repeated."

"The positions are very different," the Commandante said. "Do not be stupid, Alberto. Here we simply go down the hill to the road, then a little to the right, and there the car is waiting with Juanito."

Alberto sighed.

"I would walk very far ahead of you, Commandante," the Italian said again. He made the offer apologetically but insistently. Why shouldn't he walk with us? I thought, I'd much rather he did. Three, I thought, is a nice number at a war where there is an outstanding scarcity of women. I had a notion that the Commandante would go Italian on me again, with the moon and all.

A Sense of Direction

"Let him come if he would enjoy the exercise," I said.
"It is that they do not trust me."
What is this, I thought, group chivalry or what?
"I went for a little walk last week," the Commandante
said. "Not here. There was no moon and the terrain was
somewhat confusing. I walked between the lines and
came on a group of Moors. They did not know who I was
and were more frightened than I and I just shot off my
pistol in a general way and came back. There was nothing
to it. Now they make all this fuss as if I was in danger of
capture or death every time I want to take a little walk by
myself at night."

The Commandante laughed. The others did not think
it was a funny story and I did not think it was a funny
story at all. But I knew now that the Commandante would
surely refuse to take a guide. He was not going to admit
that he wandered around the lines, like a loon, at night.
It would not do. It would look very inefficient. I only
hoped he was right about these positions and all we had
to do was go down a hill and find a road. I knew I would
be no help.

They said good night to me and Alberto said good
night rather crossly to the Commandante.

"Do not behave like an old hen, Alberto," the Commandante laughed. "You should be transferred to take
charge of a rest camp for children. You are nothing but
a nervous woman." Alberto made a grumpy snorting
sound.

It was all right for a little while; we walked on a road which was clear enough in the moonlight. Then the road swung around to the right and the Commandante said, with assurance, that to the right were the enemy lines so all we had to do was turn left. He jumped over a narrow trench and I followed him. It was rough going and I was busy trying not to fall. The ground was uneven, there were brambles and tight bushes that caught at your legs like wire. Then the Commandante stopped and looked around him with a bright and interested expression and suggested that we rest as we were in no hurry. I was sure that he did not know where we were and I thought it would be wise to sit down and give him a chance to get his bearings.

"Are you cold?"

"No," I said.

"Sit on my coat." He opened his sheepskin coat and spread one side of it for me and I sat down and that put us in a very cosy position. I was thinking of two things at once. How bored or how lonely is he, how serious can this get? I wondered. And then, intently: where are we anyhow? We had been walking for at least twenty minutes; I wouldn't even know how to get back to that place under the trees where we had eaten. And where was that hill we were supposed to go down; and where was the road? We seemed to be on top of a hill and all around were other hills. You could not see more than thirty feet ahead, a whitish shadowed ground, with humps of bushes very soft-seeming until you tripped on them and then farther on more trees and more trees again.

"Giorgio!" I said, as best I could. Then with some asperity, "Haven't you got a wife?"

I was ashamed of myself at once. Of course he would have a wife; they all did. And what of it? It was none of my business. Who knew what they had gone through in exile with their wives; who knew now how unquiet they were in their hearts, wondering about their homeless wives, worrying about the money they did not have to send back, worrying about the letters which did not come or came and said little or said too much. It was absolutely none of my business. This war was not a vacation. They came because they had to, they came for reasons I could only admire and if they had to have a night off now and again it was perfectly proper and I should not have started talking about wives.

"I'm sorry," I said.

He did not answer me. He took a little silence and let what I had said disappear into it.

"Tourne," he said, *"Regarde-moi."*

I was very unhappy.

"You are in love with some one?"

"No," I said. "Yes."

"Which?"

"I don't know."

I was sorry for him too. This was awful. Make a joke, I thought. It did not seem funny; it was sad. He was not

159

pathetic, and I was surely no tragic figure: but in a general way it was a sad business. I thought rapidly all the old sentimental things: he might be killed tomorrow, that kind of thing. Only here wherever we were it was not so sentimental. He might be killed tomorrow at that. I hadn't invented war. I was sorry for men and women, for all of them in Spain, they not knowing what to do and not having any free choice. There was always so little time and the lack of time made everything so unattractive.

"Please," I said.

"No?"

"No."

"As you wish," he said. He sounded older and I liked his voice. "Why should you?"

I did not want to hurt him or spoil any picture he had of himself. Of the two of us he was the one who counted. I had seen him with his men; I had seen how the soldiers loved him.

"Thank you, Giorgio," I said stupidly.

He turned his head away and I did not know what he was thinking and I wanted to get back to Madrid. I would not know what war really did to men; it was not a thing you could ask questions about. I preferred it on the good lying basis: never discuss casualties, laugh at all jokes, keep plenty of cigarettes handy to give away. I did not want to know about this man. There was nothing we could do for each other. In the moonlight I saw his mouth, bitter and curved-down, and I knew that not because of me but for all the reasons, all the reasons that were five years old at least by now, he was sick with his loneliness as you could be nausea-sick with an old wound.

"Shall we go?" I asked. I got up first; he could not move with me pinning down his coat.

"Well," he said cheerfully, as if there had been no questions and answers between us, "*voyons*. Where shall we go now?"

Oh, boy, I thought, this is the kind of thing you could dream if you'd eaten too much codfish after a hard day: wandering around somewhere, possibly between the lines, at night.

"They said to go down a hill."

"This way," he said.

You certainly had no feeling of going downhill or up-hill; you just slogged along discovering incredible numbers of small holes in which your feet would catch, and taking a violent personal dislike to the bushes. I thought we were making a lot of noise. We were the only noise. If some one would let off his rifle at a shadow, if only some one would begin mowing down bushes with a machine gun. If there was any noise at all you would be able to get an idea of where you were.

"Don't fall in," the Commandante said.

It was another of those purposeless shallow trenches that seemed to appear and disappear, a deeper furrow in the rough ground.

"Look at this," the Commandante said proudly. "Now we will just follow it."

Coming closer I saw that he had stumbled over a ground wire.

"It is of course the telephone," he said and picking it up, stooping, letting it slide through his hand, he guided himself by the wire. Like Hansel and Gretel, I thought, and the well-known peas.

"How do you know whose wire it is?" I said. "What a joke if we walked right into a Fascist telephone booth."

"You lack confidence."

"Oh, no."

We did not talk for a while. I listened to us and thought if we were near anybody we would surely get shot at. We sound as if were were making an attack, the Commandante and I, I thought. Then the Commandante straightened up and said, "It was not a very good wire." He showed me the end of it; it stopped unreasonably under a pine tree.

"It is down this way anyhow."

I had a winded impression that we were climbing not descending. There was no use arguing. We would just have to go on until we came to something or until some one challenged us. The Commandante was serene and good humored and it would serve no practical purpose to make remarks to him.

But I was getting a little tired. "Giorgio," I said pleasantly, "where are we?"

"Now be patient," he said. "Do you see that house to the right?"

We stood in a clearing and surely on a hill. To the right and lower, the walls of a white house showed through the trees. I did not think I had ever seen it before. I tried to think what the back of the smashed farmhouse would look like but I could not remember or guess and at any rate the position of the house and the angle of the walls seemed unfamiliar.

"I never saw it before," he said, "but it must be ours."

There was a tiny sudden flame near the house as if some one had lit a match. Then not far away there was a dry whacking sound.

"They are shooting at us or anyhow in this direction," I said.

"Nonsense."

They couldn't see us, I thought, so it must have been a mistake. Still, I did not want to stay around in the midst of mistakes.

"We will go down but we will not go too near the house," he said. "Do not make much noise." He was enjoying himself. I could tell that. He likes to be lost, I thought. It adds spice to the day. After a dull routine day at the front the thing to do is to wander around the countryside and get lost. It began to be funny; it had to be something. When we meet the first Fascist patrol, I thought, we will maintain a dignified silence. Later we

163

will try to look handsome and collected, standing against the wall.

"Giorgio," I said, "won't we make a lovely couple, getting shot together?"

He stopped and laughed and put his arm around my shoulders. "Perhaps they will let you write the story first. Think how famous you will be. Like Mademoiselle Cavell. We will have our pictures on postcards all through Spain."

We stumbled down the hill arm in arm, giggling, and paying no attention to the noise.

We came to a wooden fence and slid through the bars; then we walked between the rows of a once cultivated field. It was nice to be walking so easily. A narrow dirt road bordered the field; it ran back up the hill (for it was a hill) and down towards a dark clump of trees.

"The trees hide the main road," the Commandante said. "You will see. We will reach the road and turn to the left and there will be the bridge and the car."

"Turn to the right," I said.

"Yes. The right."

I heard them before I saw them; they were not talking but their feet made a muffled thudding on the dust of the road. Then I saw them and they saw us: there were perhaps forty men.

"It is all right," the Commandante said.

"Of course. *Bien sûr.*"

They waited until we came up to them; they seemed almost shy in the dark as if they had been caught trespassing. They were armed with picks and shovels: the *zapadores,* the old or unfit, who only come up at night to the trenches to dig.

"Where is the 2nd Battalion?" the Commandante asked.

"What Battalion?" said a man in front. He wore a beret and he looked too old for this work. I supposed an old Spaniard on the Fascist side would look the same as an old Spaniard on the Republican side but I was not going to worry.

"The Italians."

"Up there somewhere," the old man said indifferently, "behind you."

It was a hill actually, and so we had come down it as instructed, only we had taken a strange way.

"Where is the bridge?"

"There is a bridge back there," another one pointed. "A small bridge. Some comrades have a fire under it. You cannot miss it."

"Thank you," the Commandante said.

He took my arm again and said to me, "Are you ashamed now? Are you ashamed to have lost confidence? Did I not bring you down exactly where I should? We will see the bridge in a moment."

"I never lost confidence for an instant," I said, "it was evident that you knew where you were going all along."

"Of course. It is a story of Alberto's that I cannot tell directions in the dark."

"A calumny," I said. "A low calumny."

165

A man moved out of the blackness beside the road and I jumped and he said hesitantly, "Commandante?"

"Juanito?"

"The car is farther on, under the trees. You are on time."

"The Señorita thought I was leading her to the Fascists," the Commandante said.

The chauffeur laughed.

"I know this ground as I know my hand," the Commandante said.

How well do you know your hand? I thought.

"I was teasing her a little." A wavering glow came from underneath a plain stone arched bridge, ahead of us. You could not see the men who would be warming themselves around the fire.

"I wanted to know if she would be frightened," the Commandante said and squeezed my arm.

The soldier was asleep in the car and the chauffeur shook him and he sat up suddenly and saluted before he was awake and the chauffeur said, "The Commandante has been frightening the señorita. He told her he was taking her to the Fascists," and the soldier laughed sleepily, not quite having heard the joke. That's a fine story, I thought with some bitterness, it will be repeated all through the Brigade and I'll hear it every place I go.

They drove without lights and the moon did not show up shell holes so that we had a shaken ride while we were still in the country and when we got back to the city streets the dimmed lights were also not much use. The Commandante behaved outrageously in the car but it was to embarrass me, he knowing that I would not make a sound with the chauffeur and the soldier there, so obviously listening, and I began to feel as if I were slapping at a swarm of mosquitoes and I got flustered and cross and finally I said in French, furiously, "Giorgio, you are a monster."

He laughed all the way back to the hotel and I knew he had forgotten the hillside and whatever damage had been done to his dignity or whatever disappointment he might feel and that I could come to his front whenever I wanted to, though of course I would have to say that he had known where he was going when he walked me to the car and that I had been frightened by his only seeming to be lost.

He kissed my hand as we stood beside the sandbags that protected the hotel doorway and I thanked him for a lovely evening and also for the exercise and he said it was nothing and not to get hit by a shell.

There was a line of light underneath Fred Lawrence's door and I knocked and went in. He was reading in bed and could not see me clearly in the shadows by the door.

"Is that you?" he said. "Come in."

"Did you have a good day?" I asked.

"Not very. There wasn't anything doing. By the time we got out there it was quiet."

I felt better.

"I was worried about you," he said.

I felt much better.

"The concierge said you had gone out to Giorgio's front. It isn't a good place. Besides Giorgio is not practical."

"No," I said, with feeling. "We got lost coming down to the car. For about two hours."

"He probably did it on purpose."

"He didn't do it on purpose. He was lost."

"Did he try anything?"

"Of course not." I was delighted.

"We had a big shelling here at six-thirty when the movies closed. Two women got hit at that first movie up the Gran Via."

"Oh."

"Did you have fun?"

"The food was good."

"Get a story?"

"No. I don't think so. Nothing happened."

"There's nothing happening around here. I thought we might go to the Cordova front. The country's lovely."

"That would be fine. Who's going?"

"Oh, I don't know. It depends if we can get transport. You and me and Lewis maybe."

Getting taken to the Cordova front was more than getting taken to the street overlooking the Casa de Campo.

"I'm tired," I said. "It was quite a walk getting down to the car. See you in the morning."

"Good night. Would you open my windows? Now I

know you're back all right, I guess I'll sleep. They'll probably wake us up early."

There was no hot water naturally and I washed as much as I could bear to, dabbing at the new scratches with cold water and throwing some of it unwillingly on my face. I hope this war lasts long enough for him to say something, I thought. I pulled the covers up and tried to fasten down the slippery red quilt that I had bought last month. What an awful thing to think, I said to myself, I've been here too long already. Or maybe it was that way for every one. Maybe you could not survive a war if you really thought about it, thought about what it meant and who suffered and the dead. Maybe you could only last out a war if you just bumbled through every day, wondering and worrying about small personal things. I slept long before I could follow that idea through and besides I would not have reached any important or useful conclusions.

It was dark and I did not know what had happened but I was out of bed as if I had been blown out and I found my slippers and grabbed my coat off the chair, though still asleep, and I had a confused impression of many little glass bells ringing and then it came again, what had waked me, the round incoming wide crushing boom. In the square, I thought, must be. My windows were open so the panes would not shatter and there were no lights to turn off. I walked out into the hall.

Everybody was there, standing on the gallery above the inner patio. They looked sleep-sticky and mussed and bewildered. Up above, the whores were streaming from the front of the hotel towards the safer rooms at the back with sheepish and half-awake soldiers following them slowly. You could see them by leaning out over the balcony rail and looking upwards. They were very funny to see. We were funny too. The hotel shook and in between the high crying of the women, the grumbles of the soldiers, the half-finished jokes of the journalists waiting in the hall, you could hear the pointed scream of the shells that passed overhead.

"What time is it?" Thompson asked.

Fred Lawrence had his watch on. "Five o'clock."

"Too early," Liz Bourke said. "Why can't they wait until seven anyhow?"

Bob Lewis yawned very loudly, in a brief silence between shells. He was wearing a sheepskin coat over maroon satin pajamas. "Ho," he said, yawning and stretching, "and so begins another day."

It stopped in about ten minutes and we all said good night to each other politely and went back to bed.

Summer Resort

THE FRENCH BOY swam the breast stroke and talked about love in a professional way. I swam the breast stroke too; it was good exercise and you got such a fine view. Near the shore there were the usual lemon peels, old rags, fish skeletons, and water-sogged dirty papers. But out here the water was deep and clean and the sun made a wavering honeycomb pattern through it. To our left Calvi rose from the sea, too picturesque, too Corsican. The straight houses leaned against each other with a studied air of age and their pale colors and the faded green shutters seemed all painted on for the summer trade. The old citadel with its thick, sensible fortress walls topped the town and from this distance you could not see how soiled and abandoned it was, but only its heavy beauty.

A small boat passed with two of the Fashionables in it. The girl was young and blonde, one of the six young blondes of assorted nationality who lent tone and speed to the summer crowd. The boy with her was the Italian with the teeth, who could dance.

"I do think," said the girl, in English (they all spoke English less well than French but preferred it), "that Pierre should not show off with that Rumanian boy. It is making Joachim very sad."

"Did you see the Danish hag last night?" the Italian asked, for very often he did not bother to follow conversations. "I asked Alberti about her. It seems she came here when she was thirty and she was drunk then. She is forty-two, Alberti says, and she has never left the island and she has never been sober. It is something, no?"

The girl made a little face, of pity or disgust or indifference, and bowed to us as they paddled past and we rose high above the water and bowed back.

"This place," I said, "is about as tiresome as any place I have ever seen."

"Oh," said the French boy, reproachfully, "look at the mountains."

We directed our swimming to the right and there were the rose rock mountains, very sharp and pure, cut out against the white sky. It was always too hot and though the mountains were good they were not enough.

I began to think how awful it must be to be rich. Imagine, I said to myself, and swam like the old ladies of my childhood who used to dip into Lake Michigan wearing large straw hats on top of their massed hair, and who never got wet above the shoulders. Imagine always having to take vacations, I thought. Imagine having to go from Calvi to Cannes, from Saint Tropez to Biarritz, enduring the endless similar days and the dreadful conversation of the other rich people.

"I shall leave tomorrow," I said to the French boy, "and I shall never take another vacation."

"You are a tragic American," he said. "You belong to a stupid restless race which does not understand the pleasures of life, and I pity you."

I said, "Thanks."

We swam toward shore and at this distance we could see a crowd of natives—as distinct from the titled Italian effeminates, the Scandinavian drug addicts and baffled English who frequented the place—gathered on the beach. They seemed quiet and immovable which was not like them. Besides, this part of the beach was three kilometers from town and none of the natives ever walked this far to swim. They evidently enjoyed plunging into the hot soupy shallow water near Calvi and weaving their way through the debris they had thrown into the sea the day before.

We came out on the sand near the crowd. I started to walk back to town. The French boy stopped beside a very dark hairy fat Corsican and said pleasantly, "Has some one drowned himself a little?" Then he disappeared. I have never felt useful at accidents and I do not like staring at the maimed or dying bodies of strangers, so I went on. Then I heard the French boy calling me and as his voice was loud and commanding, I pushed through the crowd to him. He was standing in an open circle ringed by Corsicans and on the sand beside him, face up, lay a man who was very close to dead. The crowd effectively kept all air away from that place and the sun was like a hammer. The French boy had changed: he was solid now and real with his anger. He was shouting to the crowd, calling them idiots and no-goods and ghouls, telling them to give the man air, move him out of the sun, turn him face down.

"Go to town," he said. "These criminals have not even called a doctor. Take anybody's bicycle and buy caffeine and a hypodermic and brandy and get back fast."

The body of the man lying there was green-white and there was sand in his hair.

There was no bicycle and I ran, stumbling in the sand and breathless, thinking what a way to die, coming to this lovely loathsome place for a vacation and ending up on the beach, with curious idle people watching you and dying like that, both uselessly and alone. I found an English doctor, the medicines and a taxi, and we ran through the pine woods from the road behind the beach, ducked under two wire fences and came back to the crowd.

Three gendarmes were standing about, as curious and helpless as every one else. There were children in the front ranks of the crowd, holding sand pails and spades and watching a stranger die. The French boy was working on the body, pressing in under the ribs, cursing the heat and the Corsicans. A local doctor had arrived without medicines, not knowing what to do about people who would go out and drown. ("But the sea is good here," he kept saying. "It is no place to drown.") The English doctor who did not speak French asked me to translate. "Tell the doctor," he said, very polite and calm, "that he is in charge here and I will do what he says."

The French boy said to the Englishman, "Inject the caffeine." He turned to the crowd and said, "Some one come and help work on this man."

Every one moved back a little and looked shy and frightened. An English boy wearing a blazer came forward and offered modestly to do what he could. There were red bruises on the side of the drowned man.

The English doctor rolled the body over, listened to the heart, looked grave and gave an injection of caffeine. The man's eyes were open and water-smeared and blind and his face was black. I had seen a certain number of dead people but never one who had died like this. The children meantime leaned forward to stare and the women, with bright eyes, clucked their sympathy but did not turn away.

He was very dead and it was only the fury of the French boy which kept us all working on him, in turns. He was very dead and not old at all and wore a pair of cheap swimming trunks and looked unbearably alone with all those people about and his face was deformed by his death and his body bruised by our efforts to save him.

"He need not have died," the French boy said. His voice had never been as good.

The sun was outrageous and Calvi was too pretty and you could hear, behind the beach, the purring roar and gay musical horn of the Rolls that belonged to the Hungarian who wore a monocle.

"You have all seen him die," the French boy said to the crowd. "So now you can go home, you can at least leave him alone now." And to the gendarmes, "What are you paid for?"

Finally there was no one left there except the four of us and the body with sand in its hair. The English doctor got up from his knees and said to me, "I'm sorry," and I looked at him stupidly. We called a gendarme to watch the body, which seemed a silly thing to do, and walked back to town. I held the brandy in one hand and the cardboard box with the caffeine capsules in the other, not knowing that I had them still, and we said nothing.

The cafés along the port were full of people having their afternoon aperitif and there was a new yacht, long and black with three masts, anchored a little way out in the harbor. The small white yachts against the quai had their sun awnings up, and people kept arriving in bright roadsters and jamming on their brakes and running for their favorite tables. The Italian was dancing languidly with the blonde at the Petit Caporal and the Danish lady was drinking cognac alone in a café next door.

We sat down at a table and presently heard a shrill irritable voice. It was Pierre talking to the Rumanian boy. "But my dear," Pierre said, "it's ridiculous to go in the water right after one's eaten. Of course the chap drowned. These people will never learn anything."

We were very tired.

"I found out about him," the French boy said, after a while. "He was a truck driver from Lyons; he's been here five days. It seems he was a happy kind of man. He saved up his paid vacation last year so as to have money this year, plenty of money. It is the first vacation he ever had, he told the garagiste. He always wanted to come to the sea, he said, because he knew he'd love it."

"Ah," I said, and watched the sky go pale and golden over the mountains.

"Well," said the French boy, *"au revoir.* Glad to have met you. I think I will be leaving too. You may be right about summer resorts."

Slow Train from Garmisch

A LONG CAR, gray with dust, raced down the main street of Garmisch. People on bicycles rode into the curb and pedestrians jumped back against the house fronts for safety and stared at the car with anger.

The girl in the car sat slumped down on the seat; the pedestrians and bicyclists could only see her hair blowing back like a ragged yellow flag. The boy, driving, wore dark glasses, a sunburn, a polo shirt and a set expression about the mouth. They passed the painted houses and the genuine Bavarian knickknack shops and the car swerved to the right at the end of the town with a column of dust rising straight behind it. At the station the boy pulled his brakes and the car stopped, skidding a little, with a sharp screaming noise. He was out first, running before her to where the slow train for Munich waited. He swung her suitcase to the rack in a third-class carriage and turned to her.

"Good-by," he said.

She looked at him and tried to say something. No one in the train spoke. Sun glared on the clean yellow wood benches.

178

"Good-by," he said again.

She closed her eyes so quickly that he wondered later whether she had really done that. He held her arms gently and kissed her on both cheeks. For a moment she leaned against him and then she stood back as if she had remembered something and watched him. Whatever she was waiting for did not happen.

The conductor came to close the doors and the boy jumped from the train and stood on the quai. He waved to her. The train was moving and she ran to a window to see—though there was no time now—if he would make some sign, whatever sign she needed or wanted. He waved again. She smiled at him, as a child would who has hurt itself and for one dazed moment is trying to be brave. She turned from the window and crossed the aisle to her own seat, put her hand over her eyes, leaned her head against the hot windowpane and wept.

The people in the third-class carriage had watched this in silence. Even now, no one dared speak lest any words seem careless to the girl. A woman, sitting behind her, moved uneasily and searched through her handbag for nothing. A man across the aisle suddenly stood up and opened his window. He stared out of it, turning his whole body sideways so that the girl could be alone. He was a man of about forty with a face like all the faces you pass on the street. He kept thinking to himself that he was lucky: he was quiet, he had his little job and his wife was a good woman if neither beautiful nor exciting, and the children were obedient. For one week each year he could go climbing (not the highest mountains of course). That was enough. Life was easier for the plain people. The girl had fine wrists and ankles, he had seen this when she was standing in the aisle looking at her man; and her skin was as smooth and gold as the most expensive honey. Better to be sure of everything, he thought. He could not see her now, but just one moment before he turned away he had seen her shoulders, twisted and narrowed, and how rigidly she held them. He had fallen last year when climbing and broken his arm: he remembered the pain and how he held himself cramped, tight, to keep from crying out.

The woman behind the girl tried to read her book. She turned the pages ahead to see whether something interesting was going to happen. For a moment the noise of the train dimmed as it will over a good stretch of roadbed. The woman heard a small sound; and she guessed that the girl had her hand against her mouth and that she was holding her breath to keep quiet. The woman had wept once, terribly; long ago, when they posted lists in her village of those killed at the front. Her brother's name was there. His name was printed in tiny letters as if it did not matter, just another small unnoticed death to add to the thousands before and the thousands afterward. She had stood in the street with her arms at her side, without tears, but her breath went with agony in and out of her lungs and she could see nothing.

Why did the boy leave her; why did he do it? the

woman thought. Do what? Something, anyhow, that could not be mended. It is the first time too, the woman told herself. Afterward, even if she cries for other men it does not matter so much. One gets used to anything.

The old man and the old woman sat looking straight before them at the empty bench. They began to speak together softly, with soft deaf voices, in the Bavarian dialect. No one could hear them. The old woman put her hand on her husband's arm and said: "I hope there is no trouble at home. We have been away a long time." They had been visiting a nephew on a farm near Garmisch, for two days.

"We will soon see," the old man said, but he was not as quiet as he sounded.

"It is worse for the young ones from the city," the old woman said. "I do not think their mothers take good care of them. Where do you think her mother is, Heinrich?"

"I do not know. She is rich, too, Minna, you can see it from her clothes. I told Fritz when he wanted to go to Munich that it was no use being rich. He could have no more to eat than he has at home and when the rich people drive through the village in their big cars, they do not have happy faces."

The old woman took his hand in hers. "I hope the children are all right," she said again.

"Poor darling," the Englishwoman said. Her husband folded his copy of *The Continental Daily Mail*.

"It's very bad in Spain."

His wife said, "Yes," vaguely. Spain was far away. One

did not go to Spain for one's vacation because the people there were dirty and probably dishonest and then those bull-fights. . . .

"Do you think we could do anything to help her, Dick?"

"Is she still crying?"

"I don't like to look."

"It's none of our business anyhow, Louise."

"No, dear." No, of course not. But why wasn't he kinder? Why didn't he sometimes forget whether it was proper to feel one way or act another? What difference did it make whether the girl's trouble was their business or not? The girl needed help. I'd never cry for Dick that way, she thought, hard inside, glad to be apart from him and denying him. Once she hoped that he would some day do something—anything—suddenly, with warmth: just because he wanted to. He is a good husband, she said to herself, a very good husband who provides for me and takes me to the Tyrol or somewhere once a year. She remembered the girl's smile as the train moved away from Garmisch. It is awful to be young, she thought, it is awful to hope for anything.

"Give me the paper, Dick. I want to read about what's happening in Spain."

The trees went past slowly, a deep fringe of evergreens beside the tracks. Now the fields widened and were neat and shaved, with blue houses and pink houses set among them. The train stopped and started and in each clean little station a few people got on and a few people got off.

The girl said to herself: where is he now? Is he feeling glad that I've gone away, is he feeling free? How can any train be so slow? But where was she going anyhow? What did it matter whether she went nowhere slowly or fast?

A fly buzzed against a windowpane, hitting it with a sound like hail. She had the vague impression that the world outside was green and she shut her eyes against the light.

Four young Germans wearing leather shorts, all blond and pink-cheeked, had got on the train at Garmisch, laughing, prepared to be noisy all the way to Munich, prepared to enjoy the last few hours before a bank and stiff collars made life sober again. They had scarcely spoken.

Now one of them said: "Her man must be a fool."

"She may not be crying for him. She may have had a telegram to say that her mother is ill."

"That's foolish. Didn't you see the way she looked at him, Walther? He probably had just told her he was finished. That's the way she looked at him, as if she'd never see him again."

"Do you think they were lovers?" Hansi was the youngest of them. He had gone walking with a girl in the Englische Garten a month ago and kissed her.

Johann thought this over. "Yes, I think so. But not like being lovers for the vacation or something like that."

Hansi listened closely. It was a good idea, being lovers for the vacation: possibly Trudi. . . .

"She probably thought he loved her really. You know, for a long time. I'm sorry for women," Johann said, and looked at the others to see whether they would think him soft for saying that.

"Anyhow," Karl said, "when we get to Munich I'm going to offer to help her with her bag. There won't be anybody to meet her."

The girl thought to herself with wonder; but I have a pain inside me, a real pain. I didn't think it could hurt in my body too. Just because he doesn't want me and I don't know where to go. As for the winter. She felt the tears in her eyes again and rubbed the back of her hand across them. She had decided that this winter was not going to be gray and smoky, full of colds and sore throats and boring engagements. This winter there would be snow (without soot) and a high cold blue sky and every one would be gay and happy to live. It would be unlike any other winter. They would be married then. The sun made her hair silver and lay hot on her hands.

Far back, at the end of the carriage, a girl in peasant dress sat close to a young man and held his arm against her side.

"Don't ever take me to a train and go away," she said. "Don't ever do it. I'd die." Her wedding ring was wide and new and brighter than gold.

I'm ugly with crying, the girl thought, and with not being wanted. She was not used to being ugly. There had been no reason for it before. She sat quietly for a moment and the train went slowly through the outskirts of Munich, with the tracks coming together and the houses closing in. She opened her bag and fumbled in it. At first doubtfully, with indifference, then careful and intent, she rouged her lips, powdered her nose, smoothed her eyebrows. She took out a comb and drew the hair softly back from her face. "I will not be ugly," she announced aloud. "No matter what happens I will not let it make me ugly." The man opposite, who worked in a hotel and knew English, sighed with relief and murmured "Good."

Every one bowed to her, leaving the train. She looked at them all, without shame, and returned their greeting. When Karl offered to lift down her bag she startled him with the brightness of her smile. The woman behind her said, *"Auf wiedersehen,"* in a way which meant only "good luck." On impulse the girl gave her hand and said "Thank you." As the woman wound her way through the crowd to the gate, she thought: the child has learned already.

The young men stood around her, beside her bag, awkward and gentle and she asked them quickly if they'd had fun on their vacation and weren't the mountains beautiful.

And she told them suddenly that she was going to Paris: she was taking the fast train to Paris. Paris was lovely, Paris was a happy place. She had more people waiting for her in all the stations of Paris than she could possibly count.

Good Will to Men

THE TRAIN from Amsterdam pulled into the Gare du Nord at four o'clock in the morning. It was six hours late. At the Dutch-Belgian frontier we had carried our suitcases in the rain across the rails and down the platform to the Customs. There were no porters and the many uniformed Belgian customs inspectors did not offer to help any one, not even the old women or the old men or the women with many children and many bundles. They would not hold open the heavy door and if they said anything it was to tell you to get in line: or they would block the way suddenly, saying: where are you going? The Customs room was large, with a semicircular counter to put the luggage on. We were four and five deep around this counter, with no space to move and finding it hard to lift heavy suitcases past the bodies of the people in front and hard to open parcels, boxes, briefcases, bags, if you could not lay them flat. The customs inspectors went through everything with slow dirty hands.

Then we signed questionnaires, which asked us what

foreign exchange we were carrying, and later presented these and our passports for another slow suspicious inspection. After we were all back in the train, wet now and disgusted, the train waited an hour before starting.

We had already lifted down from the racks and opened our luggage in the train at Rozendaal for the Dutch inspection and we had to get out again at the Belgian-French frontier and again at Feignis when we were in France.

The train was so crowded that even in the first class compartments you could only sit far forward, resting on the edge of the seat, or wedged tightly back against the cotton-brocaded cushions with two people overlapping you on either side. In my compartment there was a well-dressed Dutchman who spoke French and English and German without accent. He had talked pompously all the way from Amsterdam and contradicted every one until at last he was allowed to talk alone. At the French frontier station he invited me to have a cognac in the bar while we were waiting for our passports to be examined. I wanted a drink and I had learned how not to listen to him. We sat at a table with a sticky marble top and the rumpled cheerful French soldiers who shared it with us made jokes about us to each other, but when I tried to talk to them they acted as if they could not understand my French. There were many patriotic and propaganda posters on the walls of the station. There was a big one with a picture of two misshapen greenish ears, which said: "The ears of the enemy hear you."

After the train started again, in France, the lights went out and blue nightlamps were turned on in the compartments. You could not place yourself any way to sleep and the windows were shut. I kept thinking: there are only five or six or seven more hours of this. The corridors were too crowded to walk through to the restaurant car. The Dutchman talked on and on, about what the Germans would do in the spring, where the offensive would start, what had happened to the fruit trees of Holland when they flooded the land as a defense (it was not too effective a defense but it ruined the fruit trees). He spoke of Madrid, where he went every two weeks on business, and of Belgrade and London. He knew too much and travelled too widely. I began to be like the French soldiers: I thought, he is a very odd character, I wonder what he really does and who pays him. He was most patriotic about the Allies.

We united in the compartment, with little looks and head-shakings and shrugs and an occasional discreetly unpleasant laugh, against the Dutchman. We did not know each other and we did not say anything directly. But we agreed about the Dutchman. One by one we closed our eyes, pretending to sleep, though obviously no one could sleep packed close together like that. But seeming to sleep might discourage the Dutchman and at last, having offered cigarettes to every one and having been refused, he stopped talking.

I did not sleep but floated off into some state of mindlessness, feeling my own body as weary crushed and dirty, my head clogged with bad air and aching from a furious and despairing boredom. I listened to the round noise of the wheels grinding over the rails and thought of nothing. Then the Dutchman said, full of energy, "Here we are. Paris. Follow me," he said. "I'll find you a taxi. We can take the same porter to the street. Where are you staying; I could perhaps drop you off. There are not many taxis at this time of night."

"Thank you so much," I said. "I'll manage all right."

"No. No," he said. "It is nothing. I will stay until I see you are safely on your way."

Sleep, I thought, and a bath and above all, no one talking. It is a curious fact that people talk ten times more during a war than they do in peace and they are not more interesting, they are just more opinionated. There is no use becoming hysterical about this man now, I told myself, after I have suffered him for fifteen hours.

But in the crowd, and the suddenness of at last arriving, I escaped him and followed my one suitcase and my typewriter to the street and hurried into a taxi, hurrying away from the sound of that insistent voice, and I told the driver where to go and leaned back to hide. Then we were away from the station, on the dark empty streets and it was very cold and I saw there was snow and driving up the Champs Elysées, I thought that wide, always loudly lighted, vulgar-looking street had taken back its beauty and was as broad and serene and handsome as a river. The houses rose in stony blackness along the smooth black street and blue lamps shone down on snow and snow-heavy trees and ahead the Arc de Triomphe stood like a wonderful dark ruin.

The taxi driver yawned, helping me out with my luggage, and we waited at the gate until a streak of light showed behind the shuttered windows on the second floor and then my friend Robert, wearing a camel's hair bathrobe and shoes over his bare feet, came down the path from the front door and opened the outer gate and his wife, Diana, called from her open bedroom window and I paid the taxi driver. It was Christmas Eve, the first Christmas of the war, as the newspapers kept announcing.

I had no idea that war and snow would make Paris fresh and gentle as a village. It looked new and smaller with the snow, and the snow padded all noise and the air was bright, cold and quiet. People walked as if there were nothing to hurry for now and there were fewer cars and you had time to look at everything. The trees were lightly fuzzed over with frozen snow, or sleek with ice, and the sun caught the glass birds in the fountains at the Rond Point and made them shine and flickered in the branches of the chestnut trees that line the Champs Elysées, and the great female statues in the Place de la Concorde were soft with snow, and for the first time in my life, in daylight, I stood in the Place de la Concorde and saw it and saw how beautiful and flat like a painting the façades of the Crillon and Rohan palaces are and how truly handsome the Chamber is, across the river. You could stand in the middle of the street and stare like a German tourist because cars came through only rarely and never fast.

It was not the waiting silence of Helsinki or Madrid, waiting for the huge and awful noise that would come on you suddenly from the air or from near artillery. It was like the Sunday quiet of a small town in the snow.

I had only the one thing to do, in Paris, and I did not know how to do it. So I went to lunch at that ministry, as the Minister and his wife were old friends of mine which meant that I had known them for years, knew nothing about them, had never said a serious or sincere word to them, and never heard one, and we liked each other very much and had many happy and nonsensical memories in common.

The lovely old building looked like a ministry inside, combining as the French always do the handsome things of their past with the necessities of office work. But the private apartments of Madame Fleury were very special. There was a vast bed covered in fur, a small perfect mantelpiece that went with the house, two overstuffed dark blue satin chairs, a chaise-longue with a mink spread and lace cushions, a dressing table that gleamed as if lighted by neon, with many bottles, many little remedies against age and fatigue. The bathroom door was open and the bathroom was enormous, white tiled, with a great bidet clearly in view and an immaculate glass douche hung on the wall.

Madame Fleury, when I arrived, was shaking with laughter and calling upon God to witness the gift she had just received from an impossible Lyons manufacturer who wanted some contract or other from her husband, the Minister. The gift was a box covered in black velvet, three feet square, with the head of an Airedale painted on the black velvet in varying shades of brown. Inside were chocolates.

"Do you think we could take it back and get the money?" Madame Fleury asked.

Then she said, "No, we will have it exchanged for many smaller boxes and we will send them to the children in the Maginot Line." This was very noble and I applauded her good-heartedness and then she screamed with laughter again, a hoarse booming laugh, and said, "Chérie, imagine a man who would buy a thing like that. You can see the kind of people I know now."

We sat without elegance but comfortably on the two satin chairs and she said, "Do you want a drink? You have only to ring. They can make anything here."

"Could I have a Martini?" I said. "Where's Pierre? Who's coming to lunch?"

"The Minister," she said, with dignity but winking at me, "will be here any minute. For lunch we are entertaining a bridal party; you do not know the girl but do you remember that young Lafont, he is now a captain and is getting married on leave and we are giving them the luncheon after the civil ceremony. It will be very gay. But we will give you the first honors, you shall be made the star of the occasion and tell us all about Finland. Those marvellous Finns. So brave. How is it there? Are they going to win?"

"Darling," I said. "Wait until lunch."

"What are you doing now?" she said. "Are you a success? Are you in love?"

"No," I said.

"No what?"

"No, simply."

"You lie," she said. "You look too healthy not to be in love. I am sure you are a success. You are an intelligent girl and you work hard. In America, women are always a success."

"Yes, my angel. I am a great success."

"That is fine, we will tell Pierre."

She went to the door and shouted into the perfectly proportioned cold hall.

"Pierre," she shouted. "Where art thou? I have a surprise, a beautiful surprise from America."

Pierre came in, following the *valet de chambre* with the Martini.

"What is this?" he said, and picked up the shaker. "A cocktail," he said with pleasure and drank from the shaker. "How goes it," he said to me, as if he had seen me yesterday and was going to see me tomorrow. "Content to see you. You are staying to lunch?"

"She has just come from Finland," Madame Fleury said in a loud bragging voice. "She has seen everything. She has met all the important people, the generals, the government."

"Fine," Pierre said indifferently.

I was a little embarrassed by Madame Fleury and I did not see how I would ever ask for what I wanted.

"How is it here?" I asked him.

"As you see. Much work. Too much work. Work all the time. It was better in the Midi, wasn't it, when we were young?"

"It was lovely in the Midi."

We had visited at the same house, during two summers, a white low house with the sea in front. I remembered the time he went to Aix and stayed two days and how sad and small and pitiful Madame Fleury looked, almost losing her voice in her shame and uncertainty. He came back from that trip, proud like a rooster, and we treated him with mocking deference: but Madame Fleury had been really hurt and no one considered that.

"And the war?" I said.

"We will win," he said. "It will be a great effort and cost many sacrifices. We will win." He started to walk toward the bathroom.

"The Minister," Madame Fleury shouted, "is going to

make pipi before lunch. Out of the room, every one."

Her secretary had come in. Her secretary was also an old friend of mine, a girl who worked for the Fleurys for the laughter she got out of it, a dark, small, ugly, very chic, shrewd and good Frenchwoman who had what the French have, whatever it is, that always makes them seem a little better adjusted to life than other people.

"Get out," she urged me, "before he does it in front of us."

We went into the hall and I said, "Is it always like this, Lulu?"

"Always," she said solemnly. "Come into my office."

"How is Jean?" Jean is her husband.

"He is fine. He is a hero. He is a poilu in the Maginot Line. I am afraid he is going to lose his mind with boredom. He was here last week. Too bad you missed him."

"I am sorry."

"He came back very dirty and the Fleurys gave a party for him, as a hero. Poor thing. He has two friends up there, both peasants, they are called 'Nightingale' and 'Gilbert.'" She laughed. "He says they make only scatological jokes and though these were diverting the first month, they have gradually become insupportable. He suffers very much from this war."

"It's a very remarkable war," I said discreetly, not wishing to be rude.

"It is our war," she said in warning. "What are you doing in Paris?"

I decided to try it out on her and see how it went. I was aware that it would not go too well. The atmosphere was wrong.

"I'm taking the Clipper," I said. "That's why I came through France. But I have something I want to do. I have a friend, a fine writer and a fine man. He fought on our side in Spain." (Lulu had always seemed fairly sympathetic to the Loyalists in Spain.) "He is now in a concentration camp here. But he was severely wounded in Spain and I do not think he will last long in that camp. I want to get him out."

"Oh," she said, in a flat voice.

"Listen, Lulu. I understand about war and all the things that have to be done. But it would be a great stupidity if that man died in a French concentration camp. Truly. We would make a big thing of it, all the writers of America," I said, promising her a blackmail I could not guarantee at all.

"What is he? Why is he there?"

"He is a German," I said.

"Of course," she said. "And no doubt a Communist."

"He was a Communist," I said. "He is an anti-Nazi. He is more against Hitler than any of you are."

"Listen," she said. "I am tired of Germans and of these noble anti-Nazis people are always speaking of, and of Communists. It is not my department. If they are in jail, they probably deserve it. I am not interested in foreigners. I am interested in the French."

196

"Very human," I said, somewhat angrily.

"And your humanity," she said. *"Eh bien, merde pour
ça.* This is our war."

"You will do nothing?"

"No."

"You have changed."

"Not at all. Why don't you speak to the Fleurys? They
are important; they have influence. They might do something, as you are an American journalist. They might
think it worth while for the propaganda."

"I'll speak to them."

"Not that I truly believe they will do anything. Listen,
little one, go home to America and be full of love for
humanity. You are not practical people but if you stay
home, you harm no one. Let us manage this war, with
injustice or any other way. After all, we are paying for
it."

"Oh, balls," I said. "You are paying for it until you run
out of money and then we will pay for it, like fools, like
before. Don't be so independent: the war is only three
months old."

"You are very tactful."

"You are a fine one," I said furiously. "What are you
fighting this war about? To put in jail the people who
believe as you do and have never hurt your country?"

"A German and a Communist. My brother, no doubt.
Don't make me laugh."

"Let's eat," I said. "Where is this bridal party?"

"You are angry?"

"Naturally."

"But you will not be, for long," she said. "You are never angry with us for long. You know we are lamentable but you love us anyhow, because we are so gay and amusing. All Americans are like that."

"Are they indeed?" I said. "Ho."

"Forget your German Communist and eat a good lunch."

I would forget him during lunch because there was nothing else to do and if I failed everywhere as I was failing here, I would forget him also, because I could not go on remembering and doing nothing. I did not love Max as I loved many others, most of them now dead, but I admired him and I knew he had a kind of courage I did not have and what he believed I believed (scraping off and throwing away the dogma, the Russian politics, the German politics, all the excess changeable matter). He was brave and he had never made anything for himself and his being in jail was as if he were a hostage for me and the people like me who could believe what we wanted, unpunished. Besides I had gone through a war where they bombed you in the cities and shelled you on the roads and starved you wherever you were, with Max, and having gone through that I had a closeness to him I would not have with other people. I did not want to wake in the night, in my house in a distant warm country, and think I had left Max where he was without speaking for him.

Lulu could know nothing of this: all she knew about war and what you owed the people who shared a war with you was this joke, this talkative foolish joke, this beautiful safe Paris and champagne and oysters for lunch and the smart new war-models of Molyneux and Schiaparelli which made every one look so trim and military, and your husband bored blind in the Maginot, but on the other hand lots of friends were still in town. What does she know about it? I thought angrily.

It was an intimate party with only fourteen guests. We sat in a long room at a long table under two complicated brilliant cut-glass chandeliers and five footmen served us. The plate was as magnificent as the food. The bride would do very well for Raoul Lafont. She was young now and dressed in a pale, much ruffled costume, wearing the wrong color of rouge, but she had a sharp nose and quick eyes and she would look after Raoul's career and never waste his money and make him a fine home with dark wallpaper and a good deal of small statuary in the salon and her ambition would be as tireless as his. In ten years, I thought, she will have one of those fur pieces, like a rug, clasped around her neck and she will have cash-register eyes and they are going to be well contented together. The groom was disguised by his uniform but I thought: he must have been eating luncheons like this for years, and there was something about his pink wet lips and the way he listened to himself talk which made me sure that after the war he would be a deputy, elected on his war

The Heart of Another

record no doubt, *un de nos grands héros*. I was absolutely sure he would survive the war.

Before I had really looked at everybody the speeches started. Pierre got up first. He wore a special face, very dignified and stern and he kept his chin up as he talked. He spoke of the sacrifices we must all make though we had not asked for this war but were fighting it on behalf of the western world. He said: renewed efforts, redoubled efforts, valiance, patience, sleeplessness, *nos braves soldats,* the wives and mothers of France (and every one looked with tender eyes at the bride who looked at her plate), the order of the day is work, work, work: to the bride and groom and to all the other workers for victory; and we rose to our feet and lifted our wineglasses and drank. Raoul Lafont, in a voice perfectly copied from the Minister, spoke of his comrades in the trenches whose noble work he humbly shared, the young girl who willingly linked her destiny with his own uncertain future, the great burden which the women of France were so bravely assuming, the enemy will find us united, strong and unafraid, the great honor we have to be here today with those two superb examples of devotion and patriotism, our dear friends Monsieur and Madame Fleury, to my wife and to victory: and we rose and drank again. The bride did not make much of a speech because she had not had the long practice of the other two, but she blushed nicely and said how happy she was to share the ordeal of war with Raoul and that she hoped she would be a good wife and a good Frenchwoman which was the same thing and she wished to drink to Monsieur and Madame Fleury and to victory. We sat down after that toast with some relief and every one felt fine from all the compliments and we gave our attention now to the food.

I was sitting next to Pierre and he had been talking over me to the man on my other side, who seemed to be some one in the Ministry of Marine, when Madame Fleury said, "Elizabeth returned last night from Finland. She will tell us about Finland. The word is to Elizabeth."

There was a polite silence and I thought, oh damn the woman, and I said uneasily, "Well," because where did one begin and how was I to tell these people anything true since the truth was so simple and all the words would seem small to them, and how was I to make a speech using those long dreadful words like heroism, Red-barbarians, democracy, civilization, victory, which were the words they would expect.

So I said, "Well."

And Pierre said, "Only this morning I was talking to Béreau who has seen the Finnish Ambassador. He tells me the Russians are dying like flies. They are not so good, eh, this great Red Army? A few Finns," he said addressing the table, "can hold up a Russian battalion. The Russians are freezing to death."

"Yes," said Raoul Lafont eagerly. "They are sent out with cotton clothes and their feet bound up in paper instead of shoes. The first thing a soldier must have is good clothing. When I look at the troops in the Maginot."

The man from the Ministry of Marine said, "Our army has never been better equipped than now. All the material is good, all well planned, there is nothing useless. I think of the great progress we have made. You remember, Pierre, those red Zouave pants of the beginning of the last?"

"We will make no similar mistakes," Pierre said. "The government is controlling the purchase of supplies with superb efficiency. I was talking with Frenay about it; he is a very clever man. You know him, of course?"

"I remember him from the Radical Socialist Congress at Toulouse," Raoul Lafont said. "I must go and see him before I return to the front."

"Yes, do that," Madame Fleury said. "He is going to be a very important person in France."

I saw that it would not be necessary to say anything about Finland. The food was really wonderful.

During the meat course I tried to talk to Pierre.

"Pierre, *mon vieux,*" I said. "I have something very important I want to talk to you about."

He leaned close to me and whispered, "What is his name? When will it be? Do I know him?"

Oh, Lord, I thought, and I said, "No, dear, it isn't like that."

"No, no," he called across the table, "I do not agree with you. Reynaud is the coming man. In the end it will all depend on money, who can pay the longest, who can buy the most. Reynaud is the man who understands finance. He is one of the most brilliant statesmen France has ever seen."

They were clearing away the plates. There would be only dessert, cheese and coffee. I had to hurry. After lunch he was lost to me.

"Pierre," I said.

"Oui, mon chou."

"I want to talk to you about a friend of mine."

I could see a quick change in his eyes. Now I wanted something. That was different.

"Bring him around some morning," he said. "And we will see what we can do, any morning about noon. I am always here. Or is it a lady, a lovely lady like you?"

"No," I said. "I can't, you see."

"That is fine," he said, very distrait. "Any morning at about noon."

"Pierre," Madame Fleury shouted from her end of the table, "Lucien says that Germaine is now with Néry, you know Néry of the Credit Lyonnais. Did you know? Imagine! We should ask them to lunch one day. Too amusing. You know him, Pierre."

"Yes, yes," he said indulgently, "ask them one day. Germaine is very beautiful."

"Oh, I am not so sure," Madame Fleury said. "She has lost her figure."

Then Germaine was gone, somewhere amongst the

plates and the wineglasses. The man on the other side of the bride, who was at Pierre's right, repeated what Kerillis had written yesterday or maybe today and said that Kerillis needed a special censor for himself alone, and then Pierre turned once more, though only in passing, and I said, "Pierre, if you haven't got time now." He looked at me, knowing I was being insistent when he did not wish it and that whatever I had to talk about was somehow disagreeable, and he said, "But all the time in the world, little one, what troubles you?"

"It is not me," I said. "It is a friend of mine who is in trouble."

"We will arrange that," he said. "But not here, there is too much noise. Come to see me one day and tell me all about it."

It was not an engagement I would keep because Pierre would not listen and I knew I would have to go some place else for help. But I never really believed this would work, I told myself, so as not to be discouraged. I may as well have a good time and not get angry or stuffy with them; it would do no good and would spoil the party. Only I was glad to go at last, at four o'clock, because I felt ashamed. Madame Fleury kissed me and told me to come back every day I was in Paris. I kissed her and promised that I would, in the same warm unmeaning voice.

"Good-by, Pierre," I said.

"Good-by, my child. Amuse yourself. Until soon," he

said, but he did not repeat the invitation to come and talk to him in his office.

"Did you speak to Pierre about your German Communist?" Lulu asked, as we went down the shallow marble stairs to the courtyard.

"No, I didn't get a chance."

"From all points of view," she said. "So much the better."

"Thank you a thousand times. For your help."

"Oh, don't speak of it," she said. "Nothing. I would do it every time."

"*Salope.*"

"Same to you."

"I'll probably be seeing you again somewhere."

"Naturally. I am dining at Georgia's tomorrow night, why don't you come?"

"I may."

"Don't be bitter," she said. "It ruins the face."

"You."

"*Au revoir,*" she said and held open the glass doors and the air outside was clean and lovely. "I love you very much, my little imbecile."

"I love you too, my little patriot."

I walked down the Esplanade des Invalides, empty in the cold white-gray light. The trees were black against the flat snow and at the end of the street by the river the golden horses on the bridge of Alexander Third reared up so high that the wind had blown them clean of snow and they looked warm and lively above the cold dark water. I have never been really happy in Paris so I do not get homesick for it the way many Americans do, remembering Paris and their youth. But on the other hand I always remember the way the bridges over the Seine turn gold like the trees at sunset in the autumn and how the sky is pale green on spring evenings and what it feels like to walk along the curve of the quai de Bourbon underneath the still trees, watching the water divide against the walls of the quai and seeing the spires of Notre Dame, fixed in the air, sharp and perfect above the bridge of Saint Louis and the round trees of the church garden. I do not know any city so beautiful and you can be unhappy there and notice your unhappiness less, having the city to look at. Suddenly it was cold and not very cheerful to stand there thinking of how Paris looks in the spring.

At five o'clock there are not many people in the Ritz Bar. Usually there are two or three couples who seem to have something they want to say to each other. There are perhaps a few women who have finished their shopping or their coiffeur and are waiting for the afternoon to end. I have even seen solitary men reading in the Ritz Bar. Everything was as before, except that the windows were covered with blue cloth and the room was darker. I looked at the small round or square glass-topped tables and the straight uncomfortable crowded chairs and the murals behind the bar and the dim people and thought that if it were not so expensive a place you would imagine a leftover beery smell. Richard, the chasseur, was not there. I thought at once: of course, he has been mobilized. He is so intelligent and sensitive that something bad will happen to him. Then I thought: come, come, how do you know what Richard is. Richard may be a monster for all you know. There is no need to glorify Richard. "Where is Mr. Lawford now, Richard?" you would say. "He has just left for Morocco with a lady in his new plane. He didn't seem very eager to go." And you laugh with Richard, guessing that the lady is that black-haired bitch of a Nona de Vuillemont who pretends to write books and is a man-eater, and you think poor Mr. Lawford, what a damn fool he is to be sucked in that way: and you and Richard shake your heads at each other and shrug. Of course, I thought now, Richard probably makes up his information most of the time because it would be inadmissible for him to be caught without any new gossip. He is probably in the pay of that fat slob of a Loring who writes an international syndicated scandal column.

"A whiskey and soda," I leaned across the table so as not to raise my voice. The waiter nodded without speaking. The room was too quiet to say anything in a real voice.

Then suddenly I had time. I was not catching a boat or a plane or a train, or trying to get visas or military passes, or trying to get some sleep quickly, or hurrying to a disaster or waiting for a disaster to end, or watching things and people with sharp attention and taking notes, or asking

questions and taking notes, or writing as well and as fast as
I could before the Wirepress people telephoned me from
Amsterdam to take the dictated cable, or talking with other
overworked nervous people too late at night after drinking
too much, about the course of events which were by now so
appalling that they had no logical shape and began to be
comic, and you knew that finding them comic and laughing was in itself madness. (You noticed only, during that
bombing, that a gentleman in the hotel had been driven
from his bath by the noise and in the flight toward the
lower floors, the unthinking reaction of getting closer to
the ground because it feels solid, the bath-taker had come
undried and with a loosely draped towel around him;
and you watched with delight, between listening for the
next explosions, the turning wet body and you waited
until it made another complete turn and exposed the place
the towel had not covered. Lord, I thought, am I the only
one with a brain as big as a pea?)

It was quiet and the whiskey made me warm after the
cold walk down the Champs Elysées. I enjoyed very much
the kind of life I had; it gave me a great sense of importance to be always in a violent expensive hurry, but now
I had time and I settled down to enjoy it as if time were
something you could eat. With this new pleasure of time,
I began to think of Max. Before I had just agitated around
his troubles.

Bob Hayward wrote me from New York after the letter
came from Max's wife. The prison camp was in the Au-

vergne and I did not know that country. I only knew there were mountains and it was cold. Bob Hayward wrote: "They sleep in a long room, about a hundred of them, on straw and with no blankets. There is no hygiene or medical care. They cannot keep the food down but they are only allowed to receive a small food package once every two weeks. They work at rock-breaking for the roads. This is one of the worst camps: there are ordinary criminals in it as well as political prisoners, and German Nazis are imprisoned together with people like Max, indiscriminately." I could not see how the place would look, what the life would be like, how that room would smell, or the faces of any of the men or what they talked about. (Except getting out: you could be sure they would all talk and think of that.)

In Spain Max was always talking about Paris, saying how beautiful it was, remembering the food, remembering the French as brilliant, witty, gay, entirely free, thoroughly civilized (and forgetting all the rest and all the other things they are). He would rather talk French than German, I remembered, and nothing in Paris made him angry. When the war came the French arrested him and put him in a concentration camp because that is the way war is. He had as a passport only the now valueless papers of the Spanish Republic and he was wanted in Germany: but he was in jail as an enemy alien.

Max was full of faults and sometimes he would talk with a windy German romanticism that made you want to hit him, but he was never a man to go in for self-pity. He'll be all right in that jail, I thought, unless he dies. I had seen his wound, the one he got two years ago at Teruel. You could put your fist in it; it was a hole as big as a baseball in his back above the kidneys, with the skin grown delicately tight and pale over the hole. It was made by a shell fragment and when I saw it I shook hands with him and laughed and shook hands with him again, because he had no right to be alive with a wound like that. He could not bend over (the rock-breaking for the roads worried me most), and of course sleeping on straw and being cold was not going to help him and he was not one of those bull-like Germans who have no neck and are armored with fat, he was a small, gray, fragile man. I did not know that he was afraid of anything and I supposed he would not be afraid of jail or of dying, but it was a waste.

He had a notebook in Spain, since he was a German and a writer. At the end of the day the rest of us would be drinking or eating or sleeping or reading or making jokes and taking life easy, and Max would be writing down observations of the human soul. Max really liked people and he could not help thinking they were good. His observations of the human soul, in that notebook, were always kind: they often seemed bigger and rosier than life as well. When he met those new officers who had only lately driven taxis in Madrid or sold shoes in Valencia he could never accept them for what they were, brave and sincere men who were trying their best to do an extremely difficult trade with too little training. Max would see them as heroes of the people, risen from a dark and strangled life to give themselves for a new world. Maybe he was right: but the words always sounded far too eloquent and the facts were fine enough without any dressing-up. Still, he was very kind.

He almost never talked about his wife or about his friend Otto. He was faithful to his wife and he did not know how she was managing alone in Paris, without money or any way to make money, and one night in Madrid he showed me a photograph of her which was so blurred and small that all you knew was that it was the photograph of a woman. The way he held it in his hands, though, was something to see. He loved Otto too: they were always together and Max used to look at Otto with the eyes of a man looking at his beloved son. Otto was a Jew and did not go in for romanticism. He was the best man any of us knew. Otto was killed on the same day that Max got his wound, and during the days when Max was in the field hospital, delirious, and every one was sure he was going to die, he kept asking for Otto. When he was better they told him about Otto being dead. Everything Max suffered himself, in his body, in his homelessness, returning to Paris and not being allowed to work, and being always a foreigner, and then watching the end of Spain where all his hope was, made him gentler. He was really not like a German at all, except for his interest in people's souls.

But I did not know where anybody was or what had already been done for Max or who was working on it. You never know where anybody is, in a war. Mark might be in town but he might be in London or in the army or any place. I had heard in Stockholm that Tom was in America on a vacation and no one answered the telephone at Murphy's house. Who else would be useful? Karl would know how Max had been arrested and why and who else was in jail and which official personages, if any, were sympathetic to political prisoners. He would know everything if he was not in jail himself. I did not think Karl would be in jail, though he might have changed his name and moved to a different address. Karl would be hard to find on the day they came to arrest him. I would have to get in touch with him before I left Paris. But being himself an enemy alien, I did not see how he could be very helpful as a rescuer. I would have to manage alone because the day of Karl's power was surely past.

Still it needed some one far more imposing than I. If only Tom were not in America. Tom would handle it with speed and good humor. "No problem at all," he would say, hurrying to the telephone. It was a problem for me, all right. I could see Max very clearly, generous, brave, tender and murky-minded, shut into a prison camp and wearing out there and slowly and uselessly dying.

Then I watched Georgia make her afternoon entry. In peace, she came to the Ritz every day and the war did not interrupt her habits but only changed her escort. Fairies were always fashionable during peace: they invented hats and wrote ballets and thought up such amusing ways to do your house or do your hair and they knew all the gossip and had plenty of time to waste and Georgia was a great collector of fairies, whom she treated very nicely and simply, as if they were other girls. I don't know where all the prominent fairies went when the war started, but now Georgia had two beautiful blank young men in British uniforms. Fliers, I said to myself, certainly: fliers would be the chic branch of the military.

I think Georgia is really shy but she learned long ago that, shy or not, the studied appearance of shyness is charming and youthful, so now she came in as she always did, hurriedly, with her head a little lowered and walked to a table and sat down and then raised her head and looked around her with those incredible enormous innocent blue eyes. She smiled at the people she knew with a funny slight movement of her lips, making even her smile seem shy. She did not see me in the shadows by the blackout curtains. The two young men caught up with her and sat down and began to lean and twist around, making gestures for the waiter and seeing who was here.

She *is* a wonder, I thought. What can she talk to them about?

Georgia was wearing a vaguely military coat, no doubt

designed for her by the great dressmaker whose symbol and walking show-window she was. The coat was somewhat Russian in line (which I thought was a political mistake), and it was brown. She wore on her head a cap of deep blue, that covered all her hair, and the ends of the cap wrapped around her throat and this gave the effect of being a cross between a nun's coif and a skiing job and was very lovely. I thought: now we see what it is to be perfectly dressed for a war. I got up and walked over to her table.

"*Eli*zabeth," she said. "Where *did* you come from? Darling. Where *have* you been? Do you know these people? Captain Burkham, Miss Dalton. Captain Merrivel, Miss Dalton. Sit *here*. Get her a drink, Tony. You look *very* tired and interesting. I don't think your hat is right, but you look *very* interesting. I'm sure you've been starving somewhere. She is always dashing off to the *most* uncomfortable places."

"What will you drink?" Captain Burkham said, rather coldly. Captain Burkham did not want me around to distract attention. Captain Burkham, I thought. What faces, I said to myself, it's as if they shaved off their expressions at least twice a day.

I told him I would take a whiskey and soda, thank you, and Georgia started again. She had a charming light voice and she sang rather than talked, so that her sentences rose and fell several times and often ended high.

"Why haven't you *telephoned* me? You are very wicked

214

and unfriendly. I know you have been in Paris all winter but you do not like your old friends any more. You disapprove of us. Do you like the war? Isn't it *lovely* the way the Ritz has become so mysterious without any lights?"

"How is Louis?" I asked.

"Oh, darling, he has a *hundred* maps. All with pins in them. We are *terribly* busy with our maps."

"Are you having any fun?"

"Oh, *yes*. So many new people. And so much time now that nobody works or does anything."

"It's fun for Georgia," Captain Merrivel put in unexpectedly. "But it isn't any fun for the chaps up in the Maginot. It's ghastly boring for them."

"But no, darling," Georgia said. "They're not bored at all. They're all knitting sweaters for their evacuated families."

"Really," Captain Burkham said.

"But, darling, they are," Georgia insisted, turning the vast blue eyes on him. "They're *frightfully* busy."

Good old Georgia, I thought, she keeps her brain secret and safe under the newest, smartest hat and she is not fooled by any one or by herself. She can even make that pompous vanity-ridden husband of hers seem brilliant. And then I suddenly remembered: Louis is a deputy. Maybe I could interest Georgia in Max.

"How's every one?" I said. Every one would mean the ten people we knew in common.

"Fine, darling, all complaining like *mad* and desperately happy really. Some of course have to leave town for a while and go with the army, but they always keep popping back, looking fine I *must* say, much better than before. Every one's *so* important, you wouldn't believe it, and they all know so much. You know, they know how many soldiers the Germans have everywhere and what kinds of planes and everything. They talk *even* more than they used to, but they're all fine. I like the clothes so much this year; and I've got a bicycle, though why I don't know, as it's *dangerous* to ride and there's plenty of petrol for everybody, but now we have patriotic bicycles. That plump Lucy Monville started it all and of course we *had* to show we could do whatever she could do."

The British officers were getting a little restless.

"Georgia," I said, wondering if this would work, "how does one get pals out of jail?"

"Oh," she said and became really vague. "That's *very* difficult, Elizabeth. There's really no one who's interested in *that* kind of work. I think they just have to wait in jail and be as comfortable as they can until the war's over and then they get out by themselves. I suppose you mean Germans?"

"Yes."

"Well, darling, if I were you I'd go to Potin's and get a *lot* of food and send it, and go to Smith's and buy all the *best* books and things, and then they'll manage in jail as comfortably as possible and later, when the war's over, they'll just *leave*. That's what Louis says," she added brilliantly, thus covering Louis. "Quite a few people have come to Louis, wanting to get their friends out of jail, but he says it's too soon. And then nobody knows the police, you know, you don't meet them anywhere, it isn't like the Minister of Public Instruction and people like that who you see everywhere."

"I see," I said. I knew that Georgia understood what I meant and wanted and I knew also that she was, in her own way, telling me not to bother her about it and not to bother Louis. There were of course a great many other Germans besides Max. So the matter has come up before and Georgia and Louis aren't fooling with it. But they both love to wangle things: it must be almost impossible to get people out of jail or else it must be very unpopular to try. Probably that was it.

"I've got to go," I said. "Shall I see you before I leave?"

"But *where* are you going? Didn't you come for the war?"

"No. I'm going back to America."

"But darling, *where* have you been? What *are* you doing now, just crossing the ocean backwards and forwards?"

"I've been in Finland," I said. "And I've finished what I had to do, so I'm going home. There's no sense hanging around here. There's no story. You can't go on writing about how there are no lights, forever. I'll be back in the spring when it starts."

"Finland," Georgia said. "Louis and I went there one summer, I can't think why. *Such* an ugly country."

"Ugly as hell," I said pleasantly. The houses were red, square and tidy against the snow and there were lakes everywhere, like the small odd-shaped lakes on a map. When they froze they looked glassy and green and when there was no ice they were black as the pine trees. In Karelia the narrow icy roads did not disturb the forest. There were only trees forever and the darkness of trees and the huge granite boulders lying thick over the ground, furry with snow. Finland is not ugly at all.

"How's their war?" she said, but you could see she only asked from politeness and nothing would bore her more than to be told.

"Okay," I said. "Though they'll lose, I suppose. I'll telephone you, shall I?"

"No. Come to dinner tomorrow. Lulu's coming and some others. That *evil* Marie-Claude who's in love with Louis and some others. You must tell Louis all about Finland. Will you?"

"I'll telephone. Good-by, darling."

I thanked the two captains for the drink and shook hands. They were glad to see me go. They wanted Georgia to themselves. But what does she talk to them about, I wondered.

It was night outside and the blue lights in the Place de la Concorde made the snow seem purple and there were no cars and no people and I stood by the Obelisk and looked at it all and it was beautiful enough to break your heart.

Cars passed with their faint lights like the shining night eyes of an animal. The trees would come on you out of the night as if they moved, and seen this way, high and sudden and thick, they had nothing to do with the neat-planted tame trees of a city boulevard. First there was no one and then I could hear heeltaps ahead of me, coming towards me, and they sounded as if some one were running. I was near one of the blue street lamps, outside the circle of light, and I waited very excited, expecting something as strange as the dead dark street. I was not tired any more and the cold made my eyes feel quick and clear. It was a woman whose face as she crossed the edge of light was a bluish smear between her hat and her coat collar. Probably she was going home from her work in a shop farther up the Champs Elysées. She did not look any stranger than that. She walked fast as if she were afraid of the dark. She saw me standing there and swerved away to the other side of the pavement and walked as fast as she could without running. The snow that covered the dead grass, between the pavement and the Avenue Gabriel, was a white plain.

I did not want to go home but wanted to walk all night, listening on the empty streets and waiting for something to happen. Nothing would happen. There might be a false air-raid alarm but I thought: there is no one to hear it, it would just be that wild stretched screaming of the siren over an empty city. I could imagine how a raid would be: the buzzing of the planes coming in, the buzz rounding and deepening into a roar, the roar coming nearer and sharper and then hidden by the great almost coughing sound of the bomb explosions, and the sharp hard banging of the anti-aircraft cutting through the lump of sound of the bombs. The sky would be streaked with tracer bullets and if there were thermite bombs, somewhere against the sky you would see a pink glow of burning. Then before you had time to hear everything, the planes would be going away, trailing noise, until in the settling quiet if you could hear them at all they would sound no worse than wasps.

But probably you wouldn't hear them at all. Afterwards there would be small human sounds that any one could understand: the ambulances, automobile horns, voices without words, and some one near you cursing the planes or crying or talking about the planes, saying how many there were, where the bombs must have fallen.

You always feel lonely during an air-raid, as if you knew no one and had forgotten all the places you had been and the people you had seen and everything you had done. You feel quiet, with a desperate sort of quietness, because there is nothing to do except wait: and you hope your smallness and your quietness will protect you, you will be too little to be found, and this noise and this enormous crashing destruction will pass you over. And at the same time there are all the questions knocking against each other in your brain: where did they come from, how many are there, what kind, what size bombs, how many, where have they hit, how long will it last?

Two men had passed me and one had turned and waited for some sign and then gone on. I walked a little faster when they were close to me but now I was loitering again, in this night dream of danger.

A man stood under one of the street lamps just ahead, looking at his watch. He wore no hat and his hair curved up in a choppy wave from his narrow face and stood out, hedgehog-prickly and alive, over his head.

I called to him, "Hi, Tom."

He looked up, with his eyes not used to the light, and recognized me and said, "Elizabeth, what are you doing here?"

We stood for a moment, surprised and smiling, and getting our minds back to each other (I still in my un-happened air-raid, he wherever he might have been) and then suddenly, as if we had just learned how to speak, we were both talking at once and laughing. I could feel how thin he was under his coat and his coat smelled woolly and as if it had been wet not long ago and when he kissed me his face was rough and cold and then he sneezed and said I have the damnedest cold, let's get out of this, come on we'll go to the Café du Rond Point and have a drink, I didn't know you were coming, I am so damn glad to see you, why don't you ever write, how are you, Elizabeth, are you all right, are you well, oh you, he said, what a Christmas present.

We walked with our arms around each other, towards the Rond Point.

"But when did you get back from America?" I said.

"Why should I get back from America?"

"Some one told me in Stockholm you were in America."

"Not for five years," he said.

"I would have missed you. I'd have gone away and missed you without ever telephoning." I had not known how much I needed him for myself.

We sat side by side on one of the red leather benches in the café and then Tom moved to sit across the table where he faced me and we could see each other better and not get stiff necks, trying to talk sideways. The benches are fine for people who want to hold hands or just eat: they are not suited for talk. We ordered drinks and I looked around and liked this better than the Ritz; it is a tasteless comfortable place, done in red leather and beige-colored wood, modern, with mirrors and sharp angles, and over all there is the warm agreeable smell of *choucroute garnie.*

The skin around Tom's eyes was white and his hair looked dry. He smoked too much and I thought if he weren't smoking he would be drumming on the table with his fingers.

222

"You're tired, aren't you?" I said.

"I guess so. They won't tell you anything, they won't let you go anywhere, and if you do find something out, they won't let you send it."

"I know. Holland's almost the only place left to send from."

"It's that," he went on, "the hardness of the work and the general bloodiness of it. Oh, I don't know. I've covered too many wars."

"Yes."

"Remember all the energy we used to have, you and I? We should have bottled it or canned it or something."

He had the energy really. He would call you up in the middle of the night and tell you in a tense excited voice about the newest piece of political treachery. "What can we do about it?" you would say. You did not really think there was anything to do. "You might call Henry in London," and you could almost hear him mapping his campaign, "He'd know what to write or who to talk to. Get hold of Madeleine here, and Sam Hastings, he's a good man. I'll call up a few people. If we all blow it ahead of time, as a rumor, you know, 'A well-informed and usually authoritative source discloses.' We can make it harder for the sons of bitches anyhow." He would telephone again, several times during the night, adding to his first story, repeating what he had done himself and asking for reports. "It may work, Elizabeth, it may slow them up a little anyhow," he would say happily.

You would go to Tom's office and tell him that you had visited a hospital in Barcelona, with two hundred children in it, and they all had tuberculosis or rickets. You hadn't even stopped talking before he picked up the telephone and he would go on (cursing the telephone operators, giving orders to his secretary, sending wires, rushing out to take a taxi all over Paris) until he collected money and medicine and clothes: and then he was ready for the next thing. He found so many jobs for people that he became a sort of unofficial agency; he arranged to have books translated; he wangled visas; he borrowed money for loans; and he was never too busy to listen to any one who needed to be listened to. Every day people came, with their own hope pretty well hammered out of them, to eat on Tom's energy and leave him feeling themselves alive and confident again.

He would have explained himself by saying that it made him mad to see helpless people pushed around. I had seen him tired before but I had never seen him tired like this.

"I think I need glasses," he said. "I'm getting old."

"What rot!"

"You look a little weary yourself."

"Oh, I'm in the light or irresponsible stage. I can't remember things any more. I can't remember the name of a single town I was in, in Karelia, or the names of any of the Finns. It's that way. But I'll be home in another month. I haven't anything to complain about."

"How was it up there?"

"Wonderful," I said. "Wonderful for us. So cold you could die and no transport and work about eighteen hours a day but you could see anything and write what you wanted. Of course, that doesn't include the Finns. It is not wonderful for them."

"Is it going badly?"

"Not right now. But it will. They aren't getting any help. I don't suppose they will get any help. You ought to know. It's the same old thing."

"I wish I could go to sleep for five years," Tom said. "I'm sick of looking at it."

"I'm pretty sick of it myself."

"Want another drink? What are you doing here?"

"Yes, please. I'm not doing anything. Just getting off on the Clipper. I came to see about Max."

"Max?" he said.

"Max Ohlau. You remember him."

"I think I met him once. He's a writer, isn't he?"

"He's in a concentration camp in the Auvergne."

"What for?"

Last year he would have said, what camp, where is it, how long has he been there, did he have a trial, what's the charge, who is responsible, wait a minute: and he would have picked up the nearest telephone.

"He's a German," I said, watching Tom. "And a Communist on the books. I doubt if he practices it any more."

"Have you gotten anywhere with it?"

"Not yet."

"Well, I hope you do if he's a friend of yours."

"I sort of thought," I said.

"What?"

"That you'd help."

"No, Elizabeth. I'm sorry."

He could not have understood me. Tom never refused to help anybody.

"Tom darling, listen," I said. "You haven't got it straight. Max is okay. He got a bad wound in Spain. He can't last out in that camp. He's a good writer. We've got to get him out."

"You want to get him out and I don't care whether he gets out or not," Tom said. "But neither of us can do anything. You don't seem to realize it, Elizabeth; the war has come. We couldn't make any one do what he had to do to stop it. People like us have been running around for twenty years warning every one and here we are. I don't care any more. I've given up caring."

"But Max isn't a cause. He's just one man. It's as if I were in jail or you were."

"No, it isn't. There's something wrong with all Germans and something wrong with all Communists. If I thought they'd mop each other up in this war and rid us of themselves, I'd enjoy the war. Maybe that would leave the world for quiet people."

"Oh, Tom."

"What?"

226

"You can't be as tired as that."

"I'm not tired. I mean it."

"But, Tom."

"No, Elizabeth. Honestly. Besides I couldn't do anything if I wanted to. Who do you think would listen to me? And I don't want to do anything. I don't know the man. For all I know he may have been working for the Bolos in France. Or he may not. It isn't any concern of mine. I just do my job, see? I don't give a goddam what happens any more."

"I don't know," I said.

It could happen to all of us, sooner or later. Maybe it had already happened to me. Maybe that was why I was carefully turning my mind away from Finland and thinking of Max instead. I could not believe in anything except individuals any more. As long as I cared about Max, I kept some sort of confidence in the future. You wouldn't care whether a man lived or died, if there was going to be nothing to live for and no place worth living in.

"I don't know really why one should give a goddam," I said. I would be no help to Tom. There was no sense in making a false hearty speech, saying buck-up, things can't be so bad, it will all be better soon. They could be as bad and who knew what they would be later? He wasn't refusing to help Max really; he was taking Max with him, to where he now lived, where it didn't matter one way or another and you owed nothing to any one because you had nothing to give.

"You can't get him out of that camp, Elizabeth. I tell you this not from despair or because I won't do anything about it, but because I know how things work. Only you're lucky to be trying."

I put my hand on his then; I would have liked to put my arms around him. It shocked me to see him so tired in his heart.

"Something may come out of this war, darling." I didn't say it very well.

"No. Only another war."

We talked about anything then, just talking away from the war and from Max, but it was painful and slow. I wanted to go home and I wondered where he would be going. He didn't seem to have anything to do. I hoped Robert and Diana would be at the house and perhaps we could go to a movie, one of those excellent American movies in which slender lavishly dressed women enchant tall tough men, or perhaps one of those with a poor girl dancing in a night club until a millionaire buys her a place of her own.

We stood at the door and looked out into the dark street.

"Will I be seeing you again, Elizabeth? I'm not very good company any more."

"Oh, Tom," I said and kissed him.

I didn't see him again, either.

Then the week was almost finished. Towards the end

I had been in a sweat about not getting a place on the Clipper and then about not being able to get to Lisbon. I had to have an exit visa for France and a transit visa for Portugal and there were as always the regulations about foreign exchange so that finally you felt your head rattling with all the things you had forgotten to do and you fell into unreasonable rages, suddenly shouting when the last of the four clerks said, blankly, *"Je regrette, Madame, mais ça n'est pas possible . . ."* Nothing was possible. No one could do anything. The taxi waited at the doors; you were sent to another office. Then there was no place on the plane from Marseilles to Lisbon and I could not get a Spanish visa so as to take the Sud Express and finally no one was sure the French plane service was really going to fly. They would have to go out over the Mediterranean and fly above North Africa and circle Gibraltar and come up the coast because they were not permitted to use the sky over Spain. "No, Madame," the White Russian at Cook's said, "I cannot tell you whether the plane will leave or not. I will telephone." When all this was not done but hanging in the air, unsettled, not to be settled, I was told that I would have to get permission from the American consul to travel on a French plane. That was another whole thing. If we wanted to drown, get shot, be taken prisoner or killed, it would certainly seem to be a personal affair.

On Max's behalf, I had also called on three Americans, four French, one Mexican, one Colombian, and two English. They were all official. It was really quite quick, seeing them. It only took time getting around and sometimes waiting for them but usually I did not have to wait for more than ten minutes and I rarely finished a cigarette before I was ushered out. They were all polite to me. They would say, "I will see what I can do." If they were being very polite they would make little marks on a piece of paper and put the paper in a drawer or in a file on their desks. If they were being specially polite they would ask me to write down Max's name and the name of his prison camp, the number of his barracks, and who I had already talked to. They could not have been politer. I knew that it was a waste of time and on the fourth day I began to squeeze my official visits in between other engagements. Towards the end I forgot what Max looked like or why I was doing any of this. I had promised, hadn't I? he was my friend. The more I said my little speech, and I learned to say it with no extra words, the less I remembered Max. He might have been dead.

It was a good week. I went to Molyneux's and bought clothes. The fitting rooms were as crowded as the lockers of the Y. W. C. A. on basketball night. You got hot and stifled, trying to elbow your way through all the women in their expensive underwear, calling for their vendeuses and their fitters. "We are selling mostly day clothes, Madame," the vendeuse said.."And simple things to wear for dining at home. But we have a great success with our uniforms." I went to my coiffeur's and found that the one

I liked had been mobilized. The second best coiffeur wore his white coat over his uniform; he was giving a few quick permanents before returning to his regiment. I went to the movies and it was pleasant to come out into the early night and go to dine behind closed shutters in a crowded restaurant that looked like a restaurant in a movie about this war. Maxim's was wonderful; there always seemed to be one woman crying, with a man in uniform comforting her. I was very impressed but then I kept seeing a man who had been cried over at Maxim's; I saw him at the Vert Galant and the Crillon and the Georges V. The women who cried did it beautifully too, and I got the idea that it was something you did at a war. The hats were marvellous that winter and I thought the women looked elegant and splendid, like Vienna in the days of the Emperor, and the war was moving and old-fashioned, seen this way, as if you were at the theatre.

I got drunk one night with Didi Rouvier, who was on leave, wearing a badly fitting private's uniform with arrogance. I did not know him well but we met in the afternoon and stayed together: I could not leave him because he laughed and behaved reasonably and was not bursting with his own sacrifices. He said he was a private because that was all the further he had ever gotten; he was not very quick at being a soldier. He could have been anything he wanted, knowing the people he knew, or he could have worked in a Ministry in Paris. He said no, *pourquoi faire,* it was not worth it. He was all right up there in the Line. There were some nice men, it was not bad. "Yet," he added, and said in apology, "I did not make the last war."

When the restaurant shut we went to his apartment. There was a high white room with long windows looking out onto the river and the furniture was all faded and handsome, dim underwater colors of velvet on the chairs, and the smooth used woods. He built a fire in the small marble fireplace and we lay down before it on a comfortable somewhat scraggly fur rug, with our whiskeys-and-soda within easy reach. We got drunker and the fire blinked and wavered in front of my eyes and we did not talk. Then suddenly he said, to himself I think, in a voice that he would never have wanted me to hear, "It is so long, so long, so long. It will never end." I wanted to comfort him for being caught, for seeing his own life taken up and used and wasted, for knowing there was no escape: but I could not talk to him, anything I said would be insulting, as I was free.

We fell asleep in front of the fire and when I woke the sky was gray and the fire was a black mound and I had a dirty taste in my mouth from all the cigarettes and the whiskey. It was cold too and I moved and my back hurt. Didi woke a little and then woke entirely and said, "We would be better off in bed. I have a good bed."

But I decided to go home. The second time waking would be worse than the first time. There would be more to wake up from and it was useless, we were neither of us that badly off, it would be acting and we would not like it.

"No," I said. "Thank you, Didi. It's too late."

"No," he said and smiled at me. "It's too soon."

I did not want him to come with me. He gave me a flashlight to find my way down the stairs because the house was black-out unlighted and I walked along the quai wall in the very early morning cold and wondered whether I would find a taxi and if not whether I could walk from one end of Paris to the other in high-heeled slippers. I had that sick cold hollow feeling in my stomach, from drink and not enough sleep, and I wished now that I had stayed with Didi. If nothing else, it would have been comfortable and there would have been hot coffee when you woke at a decent hour. I had a wild feeling of loneliness, though probably it was hunger and being cold. If anything on wheels passes I'll ask for a lift, I thought, I can't stumble all the way home. I wondered if there would be good company under the bridges, in case I had to wait until daylight for a taxi. It was too cold for that. I would have done it anyhow if I had been younger. I would have done it now if there had been a story in it. I was not writing anything: I was finished with my work and going home. Poor Didi, I thought, all the time gone, all the time taken away from him and he knowing that this war is only an end to something but not a beginning.

It had been a good week really. Robert and Diana were sweet. Diana walked with her dog in the Bois in the

233

morning, wearing ski shoes and rushing through the snow, calling to the dog and throwing snowballs at the trees; and some mornings I walked with her. She was gentle and happy because the war did not keep her from being with Robert. Robert had been transferred to a Ministry and he was happy because he liked his work. They did not talk much about the war and if they did it was not bad to listen to: they just hoped it would end soon, France would win and there would be no more Hitler and people would be quiet again.

Then I thought: there are two things more I must do. I must find Max's wife and give her money since that at least is practical. And I must see Karl and tell him how I have tried to help Max, so that he will know I have not been careless or forgetful even if I have been a failure. I did not want Karl to think badly of me.

I telephoned Karl in the morning. I was leaving in two days. There had been no reason to call him before. He could not help about Max and he was not one of those people you meet for a drink so as to waste a few hours with the noise of some one's voice for company.

Then I heard his voice: that low, respectful, not-giving-anything-away voice.

"Karl," I said. "This is——"

"Yes, yes," he said. "I know. How are you? Talk French. You must talk French over the telephone."

"I want to ask you something."

234

"Fine. Good. Come to see me tonight."

"I will come to see you tomorrow night I think, if that's all right. But I want to get an address from you."

"One of our friends?"

"Yes."

"I do not know many addresses," he said.

His telephone was tapped then. But it would not matter about Trudy. They were not arresting women.

"Trudy," I said.

"Oh, yes." He gave me the address. It was out in Billancourt.

"She has a telephone?" Of course she would not have.

"No."

"All right. I want to ask her to lunch. It has been so long since I have seen her," I said, for the benefit of any one listening. It felt silly to be lying when you could not see who you were lying to.

"Good. She will be content to see you. Then I shall expect you here tomorrow night?"

"Yes. Good-by, Karl."

"Good-by," he said. I heard him hang up and I waited a moment and then heard a second click on the line. There was nothing remarkable about this. Tom's line was tapped and plenty of people were honored by the same attention. Still, it gave me a surprised itchy feeling.

Trudy was standing in the street, looking small and

humble and tired. I should not have kept her waiting. I hurried over to her and took her arm and led her into the bank and told her we would go upstairs to the lady's writing room where we could talk. The lady's writing room had a sofa covered in brown velvet, several chairs covered with the same cloth, two writing desks, brown velvet curtains and a pay telephone. It opened onto a court and the lamp shades were made of stained glass. It was a somber room and as quiet as an empty house. I shut the door.

The skin of her forehead was very pale and stretched over the temples and her eyes looked as if they hurt her. They were pale blue eyes with pale lashes. She had evidently decided she had to do something to her face, so she had drawn a black line over her blonde eyebrows and put on two round spots of a pink rouge. Her skin was very finely lined under the rouge. She had dressed carefully, trying to make the ugly hat gay with a veil and trying to brighten the blue crepe dress with a silver pin. She looked like a small, thin, middle-aged woman who has no one to dress for.

I had seen Trudy three times before. It was in the summer and she was happy to have Max back from Spain, not well but able to get well. They lived in a small ugly villa outside Paris in the direction of Mantes. Some friend, who was slightly better off than they, loaned them this house and they lived in the bony walled garden and in the crowded hideously furnished four rooms with serenity and joy as if this were a palace of their own surrounded by a cool forest.

Trudy cooked for Max and cleaned the villa and washed clothes. You would think this was her special privilege for which other unluckier women might envy her. Max rarely spoke to her but he would look at her, for confirmation of dates and places or to uphold him in an argument, and when he looked at her she was always already looking at him and she would smile and nod her head. She did not do this as many women do, agreeing with the man they love but showing you also that the man is a child to be spoiled and humored. Trudy agreed with Max as if he could not fail to be right and she was flattered that he asked for her unspoken opinion.

She seemed indifferent to people and secret, living in a world she possessed by herself. She was always very polite and would answer questions but she did not like to talk, and the moment you stopped asking her questions, the talk stopped. Max told me that he showed her everything he wrote and that her judgment was faultless. I believed him. Her thinking must have been mysterious and direct, like divining water with a wand.

For herself she had a crowded busy life which she did not need to share. I knew she painted but she never spoke of this and when once I asked her what she painted, awkwardly, so as to fill a silence, she told me, "Little things."

"What little things?"

She seemed really unhappy. I had a horrible feeling that my voice, asking unwanted questions, was trumpeting out above the pigeon murmur of her words.

"Don't tell me, Trudy," I said quickly.

"Nothing," she said. "You would not be interested."

She meant: you would not understand. This is mine: you do not belong here. Then, perhaps because she felt she had been rude to me (but somehow it was as if a child who did not want to, kissed you good night with a sad smile, unwillingly, despairingly, because the nurse kept urging), she said, "Shells. Leaves. Little flowers."

I never spoke of her painting again.

Perhaps any woman who loves one man with passion and tenderness has no need of other people.

But I had to talk to her now and as usual I found it nearly impossible. It would have been easy enough if she had spoken bitterly of the French or if she had resented the useless unhappiness of her own life. But her own life grew from something solider than anything I knew and she could apparently endure whatever happened to her and keep quiet.

I said, as stupidly as if she were a casual acquaintance I had just met on the street after a short absence from town, "How are you, Trudy?"

"I am very well," she said, with surprise. She seemed to find it odd that I should inquire after her.

"I have been seeing people about Max."

I meant to tell her who I had seen, what I had said, and

the kind of answers I got. It was only fair, since this was so much more her concern than mine, to tell her the truth. But she sat forward on the edge of the brown velvet sofa, holding her large ugly handbag with tight hands, and watched my face. How do I know what she feels, I thought, or what I'd feel if I were in her place.

"Thank you, Elizabeth," she said to prompt me.

"I've seen a lot of people," I said, trying now to work out a credible but not too definite lie. "Some of them may really be important and useful. They were all nice and very shocked to hear about Max being in that camp. They all promised to take the matter up with the proper authorities. I think at least two of them may be counted on."

I thought she was going to cry then, and I saw how badly she needed hope.

"What have you done, Trudy?"

She shook her head a little, hiding her eyes. She must have been very pretty when she was young with a pale, golden-haired, gentle prettiness that would call out to be cherished. (And instead she had taken care of Max and been unbreakable by poverty or by exile.)

"I have asked," she said. It was very painful to see. It was not that she was too young for all this, it was that she was too small. She had a murmuring bird voice and she spoke French uncertainly, with a soft German accent.

"They say that if I can get a visa for some other country they will let Max be free. I have gone to all the consulates in the telephone book. There are many people who want visas, Elizabeth. Our friends give me letters of introduction when they know any one in a consulate."

Then suddenly she decided that she could not do this: she could not afford to be sad and tired and perhaps she thought it was unworthy of Max.

"I think we will get a visa from Chile," she said. "It is a nice country, isn't it, Elizabeth?"

"It's the finest country in South America. It has a marvellous climate." I have never been to Chile. I have never known anybody who went to Chile.

"They say they must write to Chile for permission and they will let me know when a letter comes back."

"Yes," I said.

"I wrote to Max. I am only allowed to write him once every two weeks. He is not discouraged. His morale is very good," she said it stiffly, trying not to use any word that would make her cry.

"Trudy, darling," she looked up and smiled at this unaccustomed tender word. "It's just a question of time. You'll have a lovely life, you two, in some new country."

"I think they will surely give him a visa, don't you, Elizabeth? He is such a fine writer and he is a doctor of philosophy."

"Oh, yes," I said. "Of course they will."

We sat on the brown velvet sofa and stared ahead of us into the white-tiled lady's toilet room and did not speak.

I had a curious feeling of shrinking, as if we were getting smaller and smaller, sitting on a doll's sofa in a room the size of a box, talking in miniature whispering voices or keeping a tiny silence. Of what possible importance were the lives of two penniless Germans, and who was I, this shrunken, almost invisible creature, to think I could help them? We will have to talk about something, I thought. I must be giving off despair like a smell.

"I have some money," I said. My voice sounded very strange to me. "It's here in the bank: American dollars. I don't need it as I'm going home. We can go downstairs and get it out for you."

"Oh, thank you, Elizabeth. I don't need any money, thank you. You are very good. Mark gave me some money before he went to England. I do not need more, alone."

"It isn't for now." My voice sounded impatient. I did not intend it to sound that way. I was trying to talk my way back to being life-size. "It's for when you get a visa and can leave. You'll have to buy your steamship tickets with foreign money probably or anyhow you'll need some, for landing in Chile."

"Oh," she said. She did not understand much about money.

"Let's go downstairs. I'll get it for you in American dollar bills."

She followed me into the bare marble bank. She was evidently not thinking about the money. The money was

241

the only thing I could think about: I knew it would always be useful for something, even if there were no visa and never a steamship.

Behind the carved rail at the carved mahogany desk the vice president was dictating a letter to his secretary. "And write sometime, John old boy, it is very depressing here." He stopped dictating and we shook hands and I introduced Trudy. I explained that I wanted to draw out my dollars and give them to Madame Ohlau. Well, let me see. That will have to be marked on your passport as if you had received the money and were taking it back to America. I'm not sure exactly how that works. I would have to inquire. It was very complicated: it was against the law anyhow, some law, but there were so many laws, a half dozen new ones every day. I'll take the chance, I said: it would only mean some slight trouble at the frontier. The thing is for Madame Ohlau to have these dollars, clear. She must not declare them then, he said. No, of course not. I could hide them in the bottom of my purse, Trudy said timidly. Well, this is your business, Miss Dalton, he said, you manage it any way you want. I don't know anything about it, I am just going to give you your dollars and mark it on your passport.

Would you sign some papers, he said. Trudy waited. I signed nine papers. It took a while to fill out all the blanks. The vice president sighed wearily. You can't *think* all the regulations there are, he said, and no one comes in any more, every one's gone back to America, it's terribly lonely in Paris now. Yes, I know. How's America? he said hopefully. About the same. Are they coming into the war, he asked. I don't know. I haven't really seen any one to talk to, any one who knows anything. I wonder, he said, well that will close your dollar account; how about the francs? There aren't many left, I said, I may as well leave them. I'll be back in the spring. You're so lucky to be going home, he said, it's terribly lonely here.

Then Trudy and I were standing on the steps and the bronze doors closed behind us because the large deserted mausoleum was shut for the day. I gave Trudy the money. It made a fat clean roll and I expected it to have some sort of smell, like fresh leaves. She put it into her purse without looking at it.

"Thank you, Elizabeth. I will give it to Max and tell him. You have been a good friend to us. I do not know how to thank you."

"I haven't done anything. Will you take a taxi?"

"No, thank you. The Metro is quicker."

"Good-by, Trudy. Good luck." I stooped to kiss her. She looked small and cold in the shadow by the high strong doors of the bank. She did not fit into this city; any city would be too big and sharp for her. She belonged where she had come from, in that smooth deep-green German countryside, in a house with geraniums at all the windows. There would be a white unused road before her gate and people passing would greet her by name in the softest German accent. I think they would have known her a long time, since she was a girl and her mother was a young woman. She would have shy children and they would play in the woods behind the house. She would know how to play with children.

They had lived only in boarding houses and furnished rooms. They lived in Hamburg and in Leipzig, in Dresden and Hanover. There are certainly beautiful parts of these cities but they did not live in them. They had the same lives as the people who worked on the docks or in the factories and the mines. It was an act of loyalty. Max did not believe men should live miserably but if they did he would share it with them and work with them to lessen the misery. He did not want anything for himself except time to write. He may never have considered what Trudy wanted. She followed Max and they had no rest and no money and after they were exiles they knew they would have no home again because home could only be Germany. None of this seemed hard to her and she probably did not regret the rooted friendly life she should have had. But here in this city she was lost, lost and unafraid.

"Good-by," her voice sounded like an echo. I did not want to watch her walking across the Place de la Concorde to the Metro station. I would never be able to forget how she looked. I was ready to run, already moving off the steps, running out to flag a taxi and go away and begin forgetting her.

"We will be all right, Elizabeth," she said, not for herself at all and I think not because she believed it. She

ITEM 8 4497

NEW YORK TELEPHONE COMPANY
Explanation of Other Charges and Credits

appearing on the accompanying bill

NOV 1 1950

ITEM	MONTHLY RATE	PERIOD		CHARGE or CREDIT
		FROM	TO	
ADJUSTMENT DUE TO CHANGE IN BILLING DATE FROM 6 TO 1 OF EACH MONTH CAUSED BY RECENT CHANGE IN TELEPHONE NUMBER				
CREDIT FOR LOCAL SERVICE PREVIOUSLY BILLED IN ADVANCE BEYOND NEW BILLING DATE	4 85	11/1	11/5	78CR
THE ALLOWANCE FOR LOCAL MESSAGES FOR THE PERIOD BETWEEN THE DATE OF YOUR LAST BILL 10/6 AND THIS BILL IS 63 MESSAGES				
15% U. S. TAX ON 78CR (net total of charges and credits marked*)				12CR
2% N. Y. C. TAX ON NET TOTAL OF ALL ITEMS				02CR
			TOTAL CARRIED TO BILL	92CR

F
18M 2/48 CBS

was saying it for me. "Don't worry about us, Elizabeth. We will be all right."

Karl lived in the ninth arrondissement behind the Gare Saint Lazare on one of those ugly streets that look like any ugly street behind a railway station in a big city. I had known Karl for three years. A prominent and somewhat phony English Communist gave me a letter to him when I was going to Spain for the first time. He all but told me to eat the letter in case I was captured. There seemed very little opportunity for being captured either on the *Normandie* or in Paris or going directly from France into Republican Spain. Karl had several names, which is not unusual amongst people who work in the underground movement, but every one seemed to know all Karl's names and use any of them at will. The letter was addressed to one of Karl's least known names at a printing press in Paris. I found the place with difficulty; it was in a court, in a short street close to the Vaneau metro station. It looked so conspiratorial that it might have been copied from a description in a Russian novel, an old-fashioned Russian novel about Nihilists. At the printing press they denied ever having heard of Karl. I thought they probably had not heard of this particular name. I wanted to find Karl because he was to arrange for my entering Spain. I do not know who arranged it, or if any one did, but when I could not find Karl I behaved like a journalist and went to the various authorities, presenting my unimpeachable papers, and I got the Spanish visa and the Non-Intervention visa without anything more than the usual delay and ten francs to a clerk in the French bureau where they gave the Non-Intervention visa. The ten francs was a reasonable tip. I met Karl the next time I came through Paris, at luncheon at Foyot's with two other journalists. It was a normal way to meet him or any one else and I hoped I would have a chance to speak to the English comrade who had made me behave as if the law were on my tracks.

Many people in Paris and Madrid did not like Karl and talked badly about him, not making any statements you could prove, but giving the general impression that he was untrustworthy, slick and deceitful. He was perhaps forty-two when I first met him, not tall but solidly built, with a gray expressionless face that suited him perfectly. He had a long white scar across his left cheek and grayish hair and gray eyes and a soft voice. He was one of those Germans who upset all your ideas about Germans.

He listened to you always carefully as if you were telling him something he had never heard before which was of the utmost importance to him and to the war in Spain and probably to the future of humanity. It was a good, flattering trick. He would take you into his confidence as an equal and tell you news of no value and make you feel that you were at least a trusted adviser of the Spanish Cabinet. He could, by quietly working on your sincerity and your vanity, get you to do any work he wanted done:

and you believed the work was vital and only you could
do it. It was usually some errand that any one of twenty
other people could do as well. He himself knew every one
in Paris and every one knew that he was an agent of the
Spanish government and also connected with the Communist underground work in Germany that had its headquarters in Paris. He dressed well and discreetly and if
you had not known him you would have wondered what
work he did or who he was and you would have thought
he was something rare, despite his clothes and his unob-
trusive manners. I did not like him at all. I did not trust
him because I felt he was too clever. That was the way
everybody felt. I do not know that he ever did anything
dishonest or that he made anything for himself. It was just
his misfortune that he impressed nearly every one as being
untrustworthy.

But later in the summer, seeing him more, I came to
like him as I had disliked him, for no special reason. He
had no personal ambition and a deadly patience: it was
very instructive to watch him work. He thought about
Spain and Germany all the time. He thought about Spain
specifically: how to supply the material that the Republic
of Spain needed to win its war and how to direct public
opinion in France and England and America so that it
would be easier to supply this material. He was equally
concrete in his thinking about Germany but sometimes
he could not limit himself to plans and schemes. One day,
sitting in the sun on the terrace of the Deux Magots,

he turned to me and said, "I am sick in my heart for Berlin."

Usually he seemed to have an inhuman sort of brain; it was impervious to excitement, to humiliation, to discouragement or to affection. When he had time, though, he did like people, other German Party members, and he took care of Max's wife without telling any one and he watched over the families of Germans fighting in the International Brigades. But what he loved was his work, or what he worked for. He was never dull and he did not enjoy talking about himself.

I stopped running errands for him as soon I saw that he invented the errands to keep the many Loyalist enthusiasts busy and believing they were necessary. When Karl realized that he did not have to treat me like a goodhearted touchy cretin, which was the way he treated practically every one except German Communists, we became friends and had a fine time together. He would show me the latest tricks they had devised for getting news into Germany: the envelopes that supposedly held shampoo powder, the rolls of fake films, the little volumes of the classics, beginning with a few pages of Goethe and going on to tell the news of the world. I would try to imagine what it would be like to smuggle those envelopes and packages and booklets into Germany, on pain of death (but not just getting shot, being tortured to tell who worked with you before they would let you die), while all the time you knew that this was old stale news, this was nothing, you could buy a paper for ten centimes and read it in Paris. Karl told me about the men who worked with him but he never told me how it was done. He could not take that risk and I would not have wanted to know. We talked about the Freiheitsender, the radio transmitter that travelled secretly about France broadcasting news into Germany for people who dared listen. It was incredible to think that if you were caught you would be slowly killed, in Stuttgart, because you had just heard how the Spanish Loyalist troops captured Belchite, when in Paris any one could shout the news with joy in any café. Karl had been an officer in the Imperial Army in the last war and he talked of that. I think his people must have been rich in Germany. He was well and expensively educated.

His wife was a fanatical Communist, a very nice homely boring woman and we almost never went out with her. She had memorized everything from the holy books of the Party and she resisted jokes and she managed to break up conversation by dropping in her orthodox quotations. Karl was a Communist too, of course, but he did not try to convert you or deaden you with Marxian moralizings. It was enough for his purposes if he believed you were on the right side, in your own way, whatever that way was. He did not trust me, or any one like me. We lacked the discipline: we would always criticize, we would always change our minds if the facts changed. We were unreliable, with our curious personal standards of right and wrong.

The Heart of Another

I was happy to be seeing Karl again. He was part of the best time of my life and I would be glad to hear news of our friends, as well as the intricate inner world news he always had. It was almost ten o'clock and I thought with amusement that this was just the proper setting for a spy story: the lady, in evening dress, secretly hurrying to a rendezvous with a mysterious scarred foreigner in a shabby part of the city. The evening dress, I thought, would not be improved by cigarette holes: it was so dark inside the taxi that I could not see where I was putting the ash. I felt well and full of the special contentment which comes from drinking champagne at dinner. Robert and Diana and I had had an elegant small farewell party, dressing to please ourselves, eating wonderfullly and being in no hurry and not talking of the war.

The concierge at 4 rue Lefebvre treated me with suspicion and ill-concealed hatred. I do not know what is the root of this permanent feud between concierges and human beings and it never fails to make me angry. I asked for Monsieur Jensen, which was the name Karl used here, and she looked at me with narrowed eyes and slammed the glass door of her cubby hole in my face. I waited while she controlled her automatic fury behind the glass (they are paid to tell you what floor the locataires live on, I thought, and if you go up without bothering the damned bitches, they scream after you). Then the woman stuck her head out, her usual concierge's head, with the dank stringy hair and the unwashed face, and the rest of

250

her body followed, the shawls, the cotton stockings and bedroom slippers, and she told me with cold disdain that Mr. Jensen was on the third to the left and that the elevator did not function. Of course it did not function, specially now that the building was unlighted. I took Didi Rouvier's flashlight from my bag and began to climb the stairs.

I heard people talking behind the door and some one laughed. When I rang the bell, the voices stopped. I waited and rang again, this time gaily, three longs and three shorts. They could not imagine that the police would be playing jokes with the doorbell. I thought how I would tease Karl. *"Deuxième bureau,"* I would say in a hoarse threatening voice, *"Ouvrez la porte. Vos papiers, Monsieur?"* I was just about to ring the bell again: this time I would ring it fiercely. I was smiling when Karl opened the door. He was not smiling. Inside, the apartment was as dark as the hall.

"Come in, Elizabeth," he said. "Come in." There was no welcome in his voice. He was shorter than I remembered him. He stood back, bowing with mock obsequiousness, and held open the door for me.

"We are so crowded here," he murmured, and led me to the end of the hall. I had been in his home often before. "I am afraid you will find it chilly," he said, with that same false humble voice. It was airless and warm and unlighted. There was no reason to make apologies to me.

He opened the door into his workroom. There were

three box-like rooms opening onto the narrow path of the hallway. His workroom was furnished with a telephone, rough wooden bookcases, two metal filing cases, a large kitchen table and two chairs. There were many papers and newspapers and two candles burning in saucers on the table. The outer shutters were closed over the windows. Nothing was changed except that there were candles instead of an unshaded electric light bulb hanging on a cord from the ceiling. When we were in the room there was no space for anything else. I stood by one of the chairs and listened to the voices in the next room. I could not hear what language they were talking.

Karl ignored the voices. "You are very elegant," he said. "More elegant than ever."

I had been happy to feel so fresh and smooth and now I was embarrassed by my evening dress. He was going to use it against me. He looked very pale in the candlelight and he was smiling without any change in his eyes and I thought, helplessly, that whatever I did or said would be wrong.

"Thank you," I said. "May I sit down?"

"Oh, please. You see I have forgotten my manners. You have not been here to train me."

"What is the matter with you, Karl?" I said.

"Why nothing at all, Elizabeth."

"But why do you act this way?"

"This way?" he said, copying my voice. "What way?"

It's like a trial, I thought. But what is the crime?

252

"How have you been, Karl?" I said uneasily. I was being careful now. I could not see where we were going.

"I have been as well as I usually am. My life is not as exciting as yours."

"Why don't you sit down? Are you in a hurry?"

"Of course not. It is a great honor that you have come to see me."

"What's on your mind, Karl?" He would have to tell me. We could not go on with this strange aimless conversation.

"You must tell me all the interesting things you have seen."

"You mean Finland?"

"Yes. Finland. Of course."

I had not thought of this at all and now I was amazed at my innocence. Karl waited, with no friendliness, for me to speak.

"I forgot," I said.

"You forgot what?"

"I forgot what your ideas about Finland would be."

"So?"

"Yes. I forgot. Every Finn is a Fascist. English planes were already loaded with bombs, waiting in Finland to take off for Russia. I forgot."

"You do not take this seriously?"

"Don't be funny."

"This is very interesting." He said it slowly. I wondered if he kept a notebook in which he wrote down reports, saying: this one is no longer reliable. Note: do not trust this one.

"Really?" I said. "I'm glad you think so. So now we don't have to speak of Finland any more."

"I am surprised to find you so decided and so bitter, Elizabeth."

He was beginning to frighten me. He had never looked like this before. He was wearing a not quite clean shirt, unpressed trousers and house slippers. I wondered at this, earlier, because he was always careful in his dress. Now I thought: he wore the clothes we expected him to wear, he dressed for us and for the role he was playing and there is no further need of that. We are not useful to him and he is indifferent to the impression he makes. It is more than that, I thought. His eyes do not move or change as he speaks. He sees only inward to what he thinks: nothing outside is real. He does not think of the war in Finland in terms of people and of pain: it is a plan. There is only the plan to consider.

Then I thought: perhaps he has not changed and it is only now that I see him. I believed he loved Spain. Perhaps that was only a plan too. Probably he saw that war inside his head, thinking with those fixed cold unreasoning eyes. It was necessary to make me believe that he loved the land and the people. What does he want, I thought, or is it like madness? he wants the plan to work, no matter how and for no reason. The plan is power, I thought, the plan is to rule. It has nothing to do with people or how people live or what they hope or want or need. It exists by itself.

I spoke to him slowly, looking for the words.

"I do not think we can agree about doctrine, Karl, but it doesn't matter. There is nothing personal in this. We do not need to be enemies. I came to see you tonight about our friends. At least we can agree about that and we can work together."

"Naturally," he said smoothly. "There is no question of being enemies, Elizabeth." His voice changed. I did not like this change, it came too quickly and too easily. "I always enjoy how you talk. It is so dramatic. What about our friends?"

"I was thinking of Max, though there are probably many more. But we'd better take one at a time. I came to Paris to see what I could do about getting Max out of that camp."

"Yes?" he said. I stopped and waited, surely there was something more.

"I have not been very successful." What did he mean by that "Yes?" "I have not been successful at all, really. I want your advice."

"What have you done?"

I told him. He listened carefully. He asked me to repeat two names, the names of the Mexican and the Colombian. He did not know them. They aren't very important, I said, I think they're first or second secretaries. The embassy people are usually more powerful than the consular people, so I went to them: not that they seemed in any position to make decisions. What had the Americans said? Nothing really: they were very nice and agreed that it was a scandal for Max to be in jail. I don't know exactly what they can do anyhow, I said, this isn't their country. Though if we could manage to get a visa for Max, I think it would be fairly easy to make the French release him.

"Really?" he said. "I did not know that."

"That's what they say."

"Ah," he said, thoughtfully.

"So you see, it's at a standstill. What can we do now?"

"It is very difficult," he said. He had picked up a paper knife from the table and he turned it in his hands. "It is a very difficult question."

"I know that."

"There are many angles to it," he said. He stopped turning the paper knife and looked at me suddenly. His eyes were quick and calculating; he was really looking at me.

"Max is very well known," he said.

"I wish he were better known. It's the only hope we have, that some people do know him in America."

"He is a writer of great talent; he can have much influence."

"Of course," I said impatiently. "I know Max. What can we do about it?"

256

"It is necessary to think this out carefully," he said, as if he were talking to himself.

I stopped myself from speaking. I had been about to protest, saying: what do you mean, think it out? What is there to think out? Have you forgotten Max? Have you forgotten what Max did in Spain? But now I waited and I had the feeling of not being in my body, of hearing a voice twice, both in the present and the past. I had been in this same place, hearing these same words, some other time, before, long ago. It is a sensation like the beginning of going under ether and you jerk yourself out of it and try to focus your eyes and remember where you are. I had that dream sense of repetition, and yet it was as if I saw Karl for the first time and this room with its almost pretentious poverty, like a stage setting of the home of a revolutionary, was new to me and I had never been here before.

Karl was busy with his paper knife. We sat in silence and I thought that when Max was fighting at Teruel, that Christmas, and men died of the cold before the stretcher bearers could reach them and Teruel rose up on its red rock cliffs and had to be taken and Max was blown out of his body and came back to it days later in unbearable pain, Karl was in Paris living safely and eating whenever he wanted to. Karl was warm and whole. And when Max was in a concentration camp in Germany, paying for what he believed with his body (and it is surely the only hard way to pay, I am unable to pay much attention to the torments of the mind, comparing them with being beaten for instance until you faint, comparing the doubts and miseries of the spirit with say four weeks of solitary confinement in a wet unlighted cellar where you can neither sit nor lie), Karl had already escaped to France. Max believed in men, but Karl believed in a plan. Max, I thought, the poor fool, thought the plan was made for the service of men. He was always ready to go out and offer his not very strong body for the men and the plan that was to serve them. Max is a fool, I thought, he does not survive. Karl will survive.

There was more to come and I did not know what it was and I would wait and be cautious. I was not going to make any more mistakes about this man. I liked him once, I thought, I really liked him.

"I don't quite understand you, Karl." I said it seriously and pleasantly and I made my face match my voice.

"I will explain to you. As you say, this thing of Finland is a difference between us, but we are old friends and we have worked together and we can have confidence in each other. We can accept the difference and possibly it will change later. You will have time to see all the implications. Or perhaps it has been a mistake and it will be corrected."

The second or the third time you see it is just as bad as the first time. It is surprising how you can see it, when you are trying not to look. There was just a round loose

ugly gray bundle, lying in the street against the wall, with
no head. Only the curled up frail-looking hand was real.
When the houses burned, on the first day, burning all at
once like celluloid when the thermite bombs hit them,
they were exciting to watch. Fires are always exciting.
Of course people lived in the houses and later, when the
fires were put out, they began to dig for the bodies and
they kept finding them for two weeks afterwards. The
state radio called out the names of children at night: a
voice would say the name of a child and its age or approx-
imate age and if the child had forgotten its name the
radio voice would describe the child. It was hoped that
parents or friends would be able to identify the lost children this way and call for them: not to take them home,
since the homes were gone, but to take them somewhere, farther away. The children used to walk out of
the city alone and sometimes you would see two or three
of them. If you did not see their faces they looked small
and sweet, stumbling along hand in hand. Whenever
the bombs fell they would just go away, not knowing
where they were going, but only going away from the
noise and from the places they had lived in. The places
were not good for children any more: they knew that.
There were also the young men in the army; after they
were dead the snow covered them very quickly. Correct
the mistake.

"Yes," I said.

"Now this thing of Max is an entirely different problem. It is small and personal and we should discuss it together and decide what we think is the best means of handling it."

I took a risk then. I wanted to know what he thought and maybe I would talk too much and he would not tell me. But I had to ask him one question, for myself.

"You are fond of Max, aren't you, Karl?"

It was a risk all right, and he looked at me quickly though he answered without hesitation. "You know that, Elizabeth. I have known Max for years. He is a fine man. I think he is often foolish but that is perhaps because of his imagination. Writers are naturally more volatile than other people," he smiled at me.

"Very volatile," I said cheerfully.

"Now the problem with Max," he went on, in a confidential voice, "is that he is at present in a rather uncertain state of mind."

"How do you mean?"

"He has written me several times and he has written to other friends in Paris. I think it is possible that this experience has shaken him a good deal."

"You mean he's scared?"

"It may be that," Karl said smoothly. Oh you liar, I thought, you liar. Where were you when Max was being brave; where were you when Max was in jail before?

"I think perhaps it is that he is tired," Karl said. "He has gone through much hardship these last years. I think he would like to live quietly for a time, in some safe country. He has written me about America, saying it is the only country he has hope in. He believes that American democracy is a good thing."

"Yes?"

"He has also written some of our friends rather hysterically, I thought, about the German-Soviet pact."

"Has he?"

"Have you seen the manuscript of his new book?"

"No."

"Trudy showed it to me. There is some excellent writing in it though the thinking is very confused. He writes a good deal in the stream-of-consciousness style about the Moscow Trials."

"I shouldn't think that would make very interesting reading."

"No. It slows up the book. It is quite extraneous. We have deleted it from the version which is appearing in France."

Does Max know that, I thought. Would they think it necessary, for discipline perhaps, to tell him? Had they decided it would do him good to think about it, helplessly, in jail?

"Of course, Max's being in jail has roused sympathy for others in the same situation who are not so well known. It has been very effective to use his name in making the appeals in other countries. He is doing a great service in this way."

"All right, Karl," I said.

"All right?"

"I understand you, Karl. Comrade Karl. You don't need to waste any more time."

"What are you talking about, Elizabeth?" How he fooled me, I thought, what a fool I have been.

"In jail, Max is very useful. He is a martyr. He cannot write uncensored letters and he cannot receive visitors. He is the best martyr material there is. On the other hand, if he were free he might actually make quite a fool of himself. He is volatile, isn't he? What could be worse than an honest volatile man, in times like these?"

"You are determined to quarrel with me, aren't you, Elizabeth?"

"No."

"What is it then?"

"I am determined to get Max out of jail."

"But of course," Karl said. "Naturally. I only suggest that you do not forget there are others beside Max. Max is not the only man to consider. I was trying to correct a too limited and subjective view of this problem. I hope you will help all the political prisoners. I am sure we can count on you for that."

"Oh sure," I said.

"I do not recognize you any more, Elizabeth."

"Really?"

"We seem to be having a very unsatisfactory visit," he said. Why was he still bothering with me? What did he want now, what did he think I would do for him?

"Will you have something to drink before you go?"

"No. I'm just going."

"I will see you down the stairs."

"Don't bother, Karl. I have a flashlight."

The voices in the other room softened into a murmur as we walked down the hall. He opened the front door. He offered me his hand and I did not see it, so that he should know I would not shake hands with him.

"Good-by, Elizabeth."

"Good-by."

"I am very sorry to see you this way."

"Good-by, Karl."

"I hope you will think it all over and change your mind. I do not want to lose you as a friend. When I see you next time, I hope you will feel more kindly towards me."

"I doubt if I'll see you," I said.

"We will meet in America."

"What?"

"Yes, we will meet in New York probably. I am planning to leave for America in three weeks."

"You aren't," I said.

"It is quite impossible here," he shrugged. "I cannot work. My telephone is tapped and my mail is opened and I am followed."

"So you will be leaving for America in three weeks?"

"And when we meet there, perhaps you will remember what friends we have been and how we have worked together."

"Of course you would be going to America," I said. "I hadn't thought of that."

He closed the door as I turned the first bend in the staircase. Perhaps he had had too much war, twenty years ago. Many people had had too much war. They would all be going to America. It was a fine thing to stay in a country and plan, and when the plans happened there was America. At least there was America for right now and later there would be some other country. America will be crowded with interesting people, I thought.

Though of course Robert and Diana will be staying for this war. And Didi Rouvier would be on hand. Georgia would probably be driving out of Paris in the Rolls Royce of some American Princess, but if she did leave it would be because her ornamental friends were going and she had not stopped to think what it meant. Perhaps she would not leave anyhow. The government naturally would move: that is what governments do. If it gets bad enough they leave the country individually, in planes or destroyers. You can't expect a government to wait around for the ripening of their works. But Lulu would not go from Paris for anything. Lulu did not really believe there was any other place than Paris. Lulu would be fixed, hating and contemptuous when the bombers come over.

Then I thought: when the bombers come over. They

will have to come, that or something even worse. There is going to be a war, though what kind of war I don't know. And then I thought: but Karl won't see it. Karl will be planning somewhere else. He was not in Madrid and he stopped coming to Barcelona. He sent men into Germany, he organized it, but he did not go himself. It was Max who always went. It would always be some one like Max, but never Karl. Well, I thought, the war is probably going to be frightful very soon, now that Karl is leaving. You could take it as a sign.

How does he dare, I thought, how dare he arrange himself so well and safely and always risk some one else? How dare he see so far ahead? I hope he doesn't get out, I hope he has to pay just once, he himself, with his fear and with the waiting nights, with hearing the noise of the planes and feeling the walls shake, himself seeing what the dead are like and knowing in his mind, always knowing (as you do, as you cannot help knowing) that it could be you. I hope he gets caught on some blocked road with the refugees when the planes come over, I hope he lies at the edge of a road somewhere with his hands over the back of his head, hearing the planes diving and rising and diving and hearing their machine guns rattle and hammer along the road, with only his hands over the back of his head and his face on the ground, he trying to flatten himself into the dirt. Let him suffer just once, I thought, all of it, every minute of it. But he won't, I thought, he will go to America. He will always manage to leave in advance of disaster. He will never know how the plan looks when it is actually happening but he will be sure the plan is right; other people are weaklings and fools and unreliable who will take no risks with human life because of what they have seen.

It came to me very suddenly, so that I stopped on the stairs. He wants Max to stay in jail, I thought; *he* is going to America. There would not be room for them both, he thinks, because he is no longer sure of Max. Max, he says, is in an uncertain state of mind. Max usually talks when something distresses him. He writes, which is even worse. And people might listen to Max and not to Karl. He cannot be certain of course: Max might not want to talk or write or he might land in some other country, with distance to silence him. Still, it is a chance. Karl does not take chances.

I had started to go back up the stairs. Then I turned again and guided myself with the flashlight down the stairs to the front door. He would be polite, that was all, and laugh at me and probably pat my shoulder and tell me I was tired, I was excited, and no doubt he would offer to see me home and say he was worried about me. What difference would a few words make to Karl? I knocked hard on the glass of the front door. Where was the button that opened the lock; how were you expected to find it in the dark? I want to get out of here, I thought. The door rattled and I called, *"Ouvrez la porte,"* and knocked on it again.

266

The concierge banged her own door open and said in a loud furious voice, *"Voyons,* what is going on here? What are you doing?"

"Open the door."

"Not so fast," she said.

"Open the door, I tell you."

I heard the buzzer that released the lock and I pushed open the door and crossed the street to where my taxi was still waiting.

The chauffeur was asleep and I woke him and gave him Robert's address. He must have thought my voice was strange.

"Ça va bien, Madame?" he said.

"Oh, yes," I said. "All goes well."

The windows of the taxi were shut and still it was so cold that they were frosted on the inside. It would be very cold for Max in the Auvergne this winter. It would be very cold and very long. He wasn't the only one. What would happen to them all when this war really started: where would they be when the war was over? I would probably never see Max again. It caught up with Max early. It would catch up with all of them. How did I know I would ever see any of them again: this was only the beginning of the war. But Karl would be all right. Karl had thought everything out. I would see Karl in America.